MUTANTS FROM THE DEEP

BY DAVID ORME

Library of Congress Cataloging-in-Publication Data

Orme, David, 1948 Mar. 1–

    [Boffin Boy and the Monsters from the Deep]

    Mutants from the Deep / by David Orme; illustrated by Peter Richardson.

    p. cm. — (Billy Blaster)

    Originally published. Boffin Boy and the Monsters from the Deep. Watlington: Ransom, 2006.

    ISBN 978-1-4342-1269-6 (library binding)

    1. Graphic novels. [1. Graphic novels. 2. Heroes—Fiction. 3. Science fiction.]

I. Richardson, Peter, 1965– ill. II. Title.

PZ7.7.O76Mut 2009

741.5'973—dc22   2008031346

Summary:

Evil sailors have been dumping toxic waste into the ocean, and they've accidentally created monsters: giant mutant jellyfish! Now, the monsters are stealing candy from people all over town. Billy Blaster needs to send the sugar-crazed mutants back to the sea. Unfortunately, his ninja wizard friend, Wu Hoo, has a dangerous sweet tooth.

Creative Director: Heather Kindseth

Graphic Designer: Carla Zetina-Yglesias

BILLY BLASTER

written by
DAVID ORME

illustrated by
PETER RICHARDSON

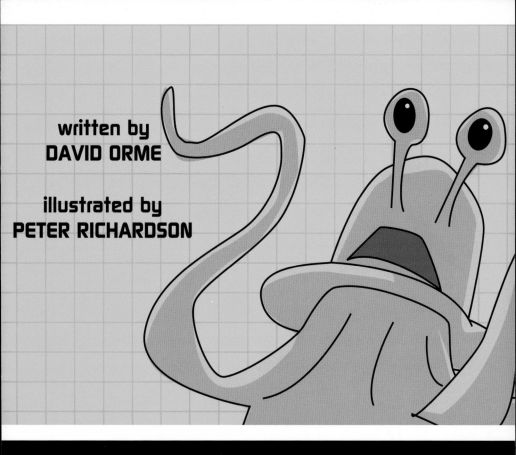

MUTANTS FROM THE DEEP

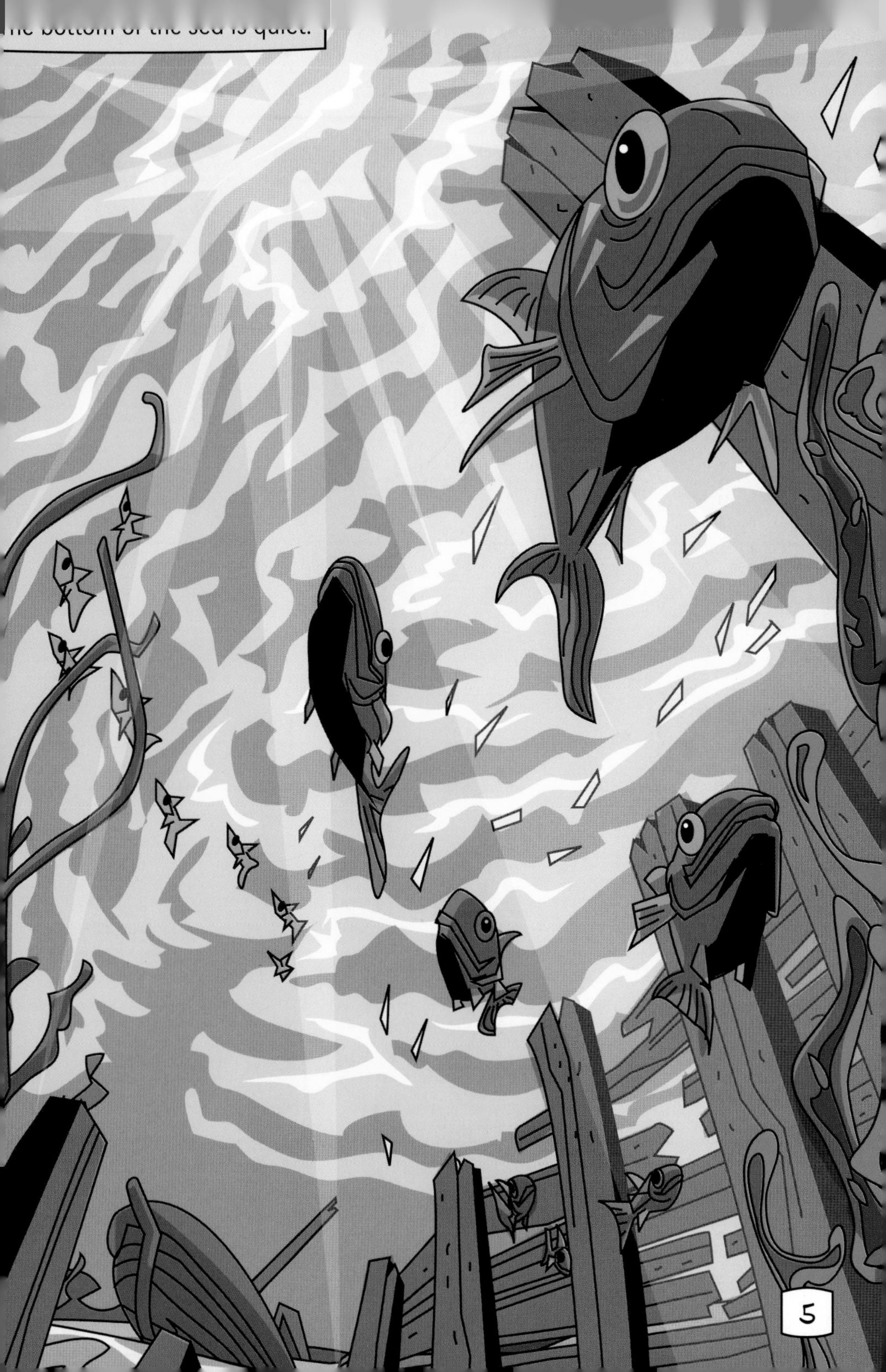
he bottom of the sea is quiet.

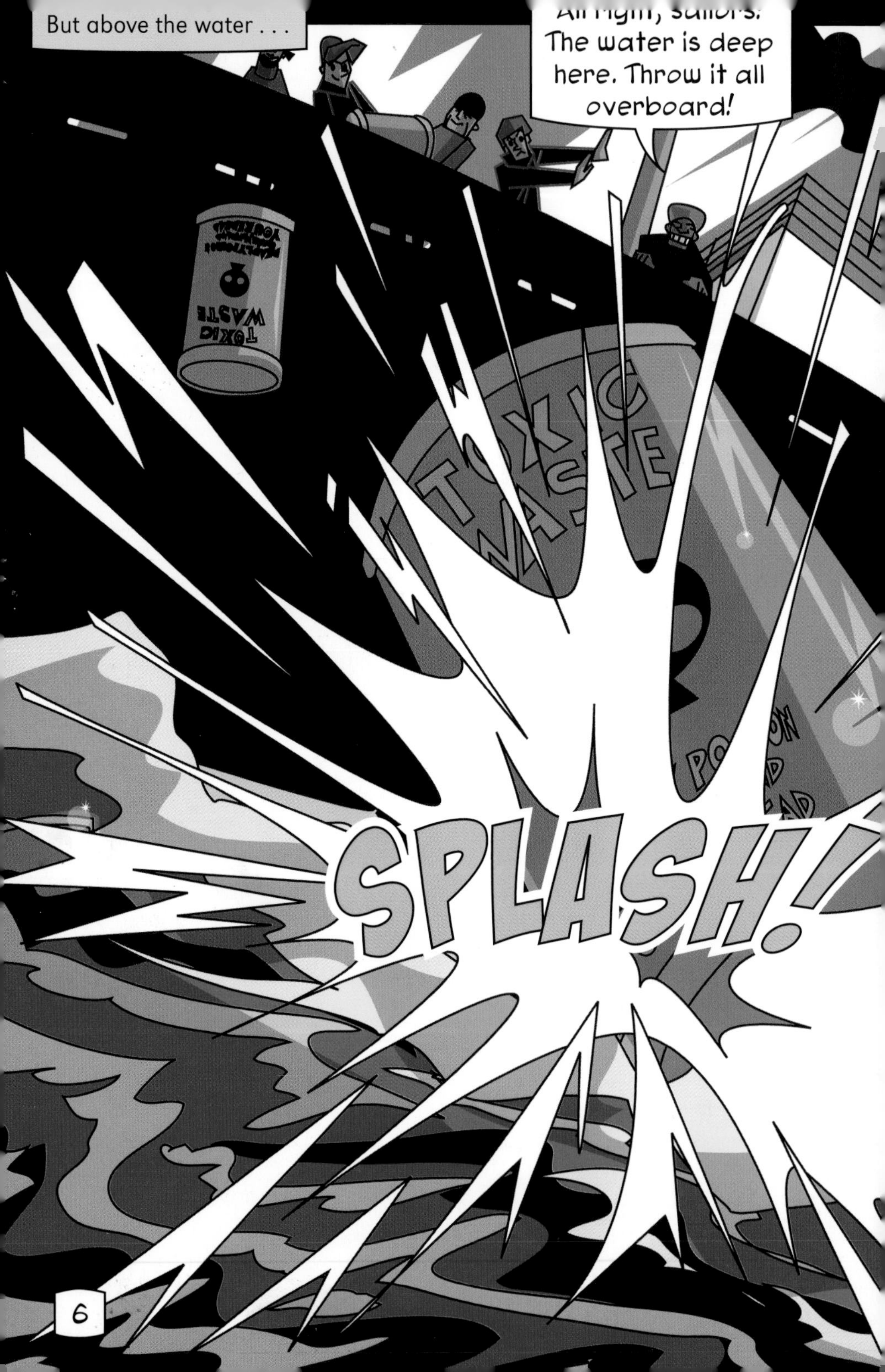

But above the water . . .
All right, sailors! The water is deep here. Throw it all overboard!
TOXIC WASTE
SPLASH!

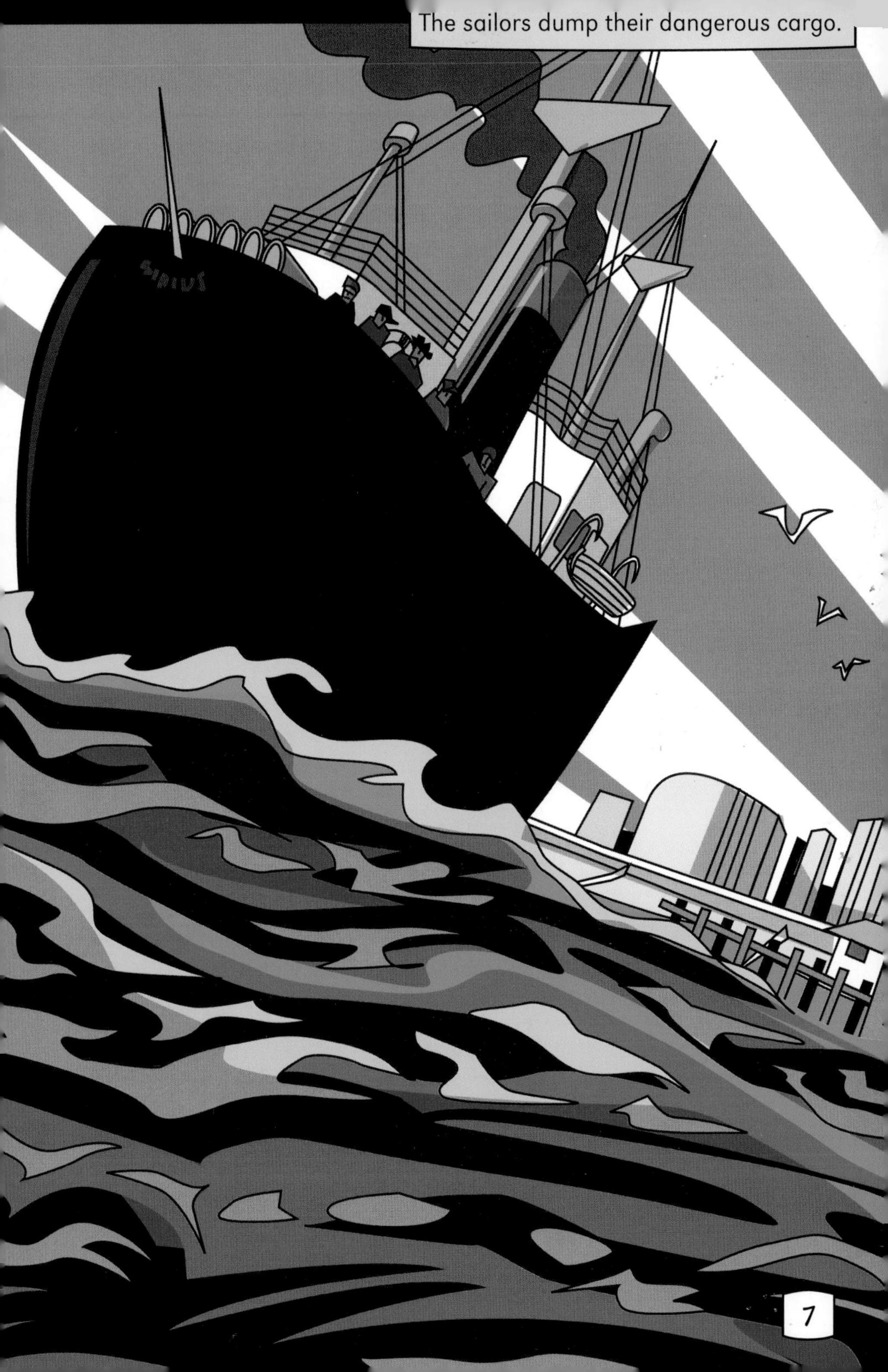
The sailors dump their dangerous cargo.

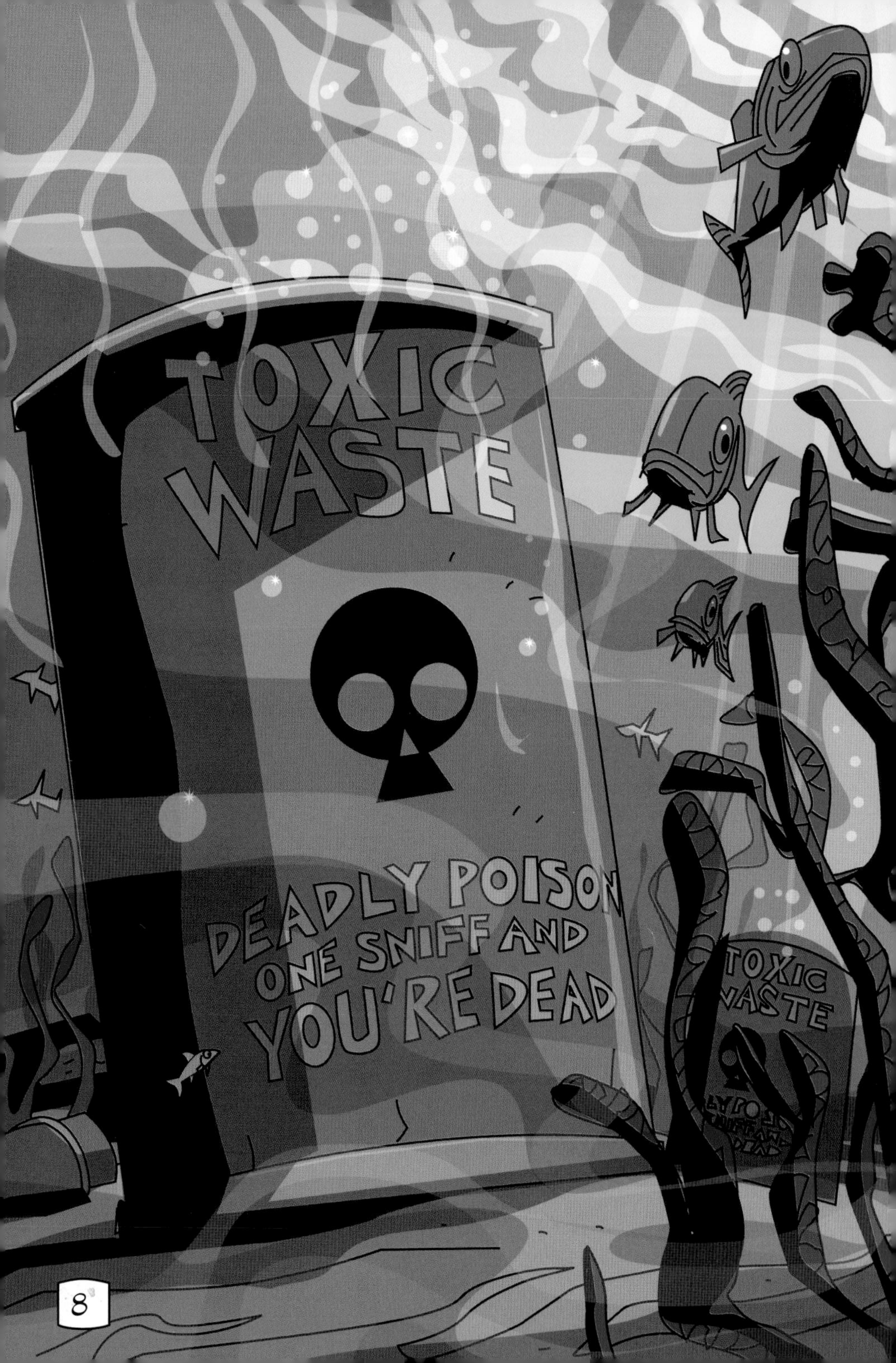
TOXIC WASTE
DEADLY POISON
ONE SNIFF AND
YOU'RE DEAD
TOXIC WASTE

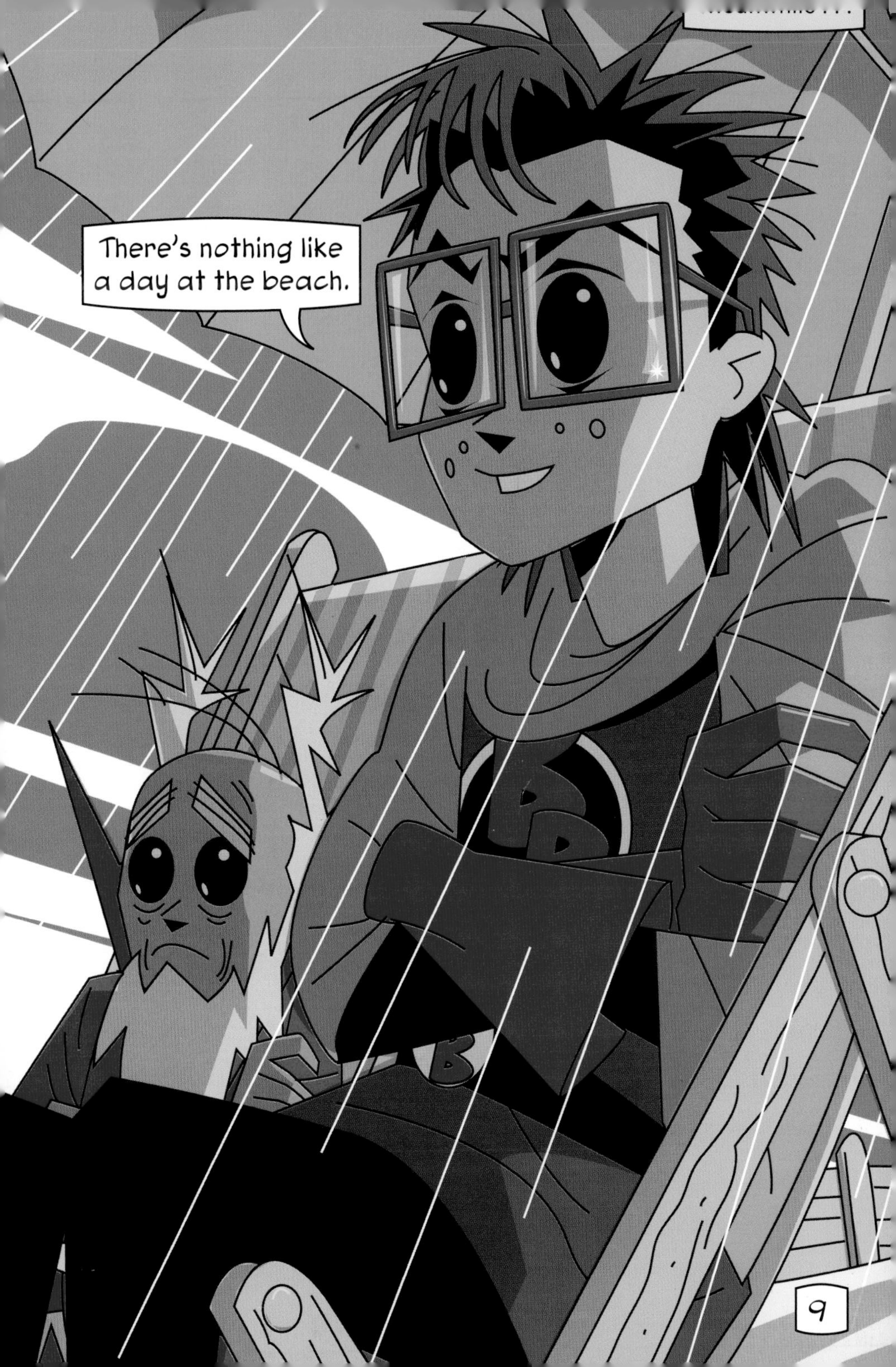
There's nothing like a day at the beach.

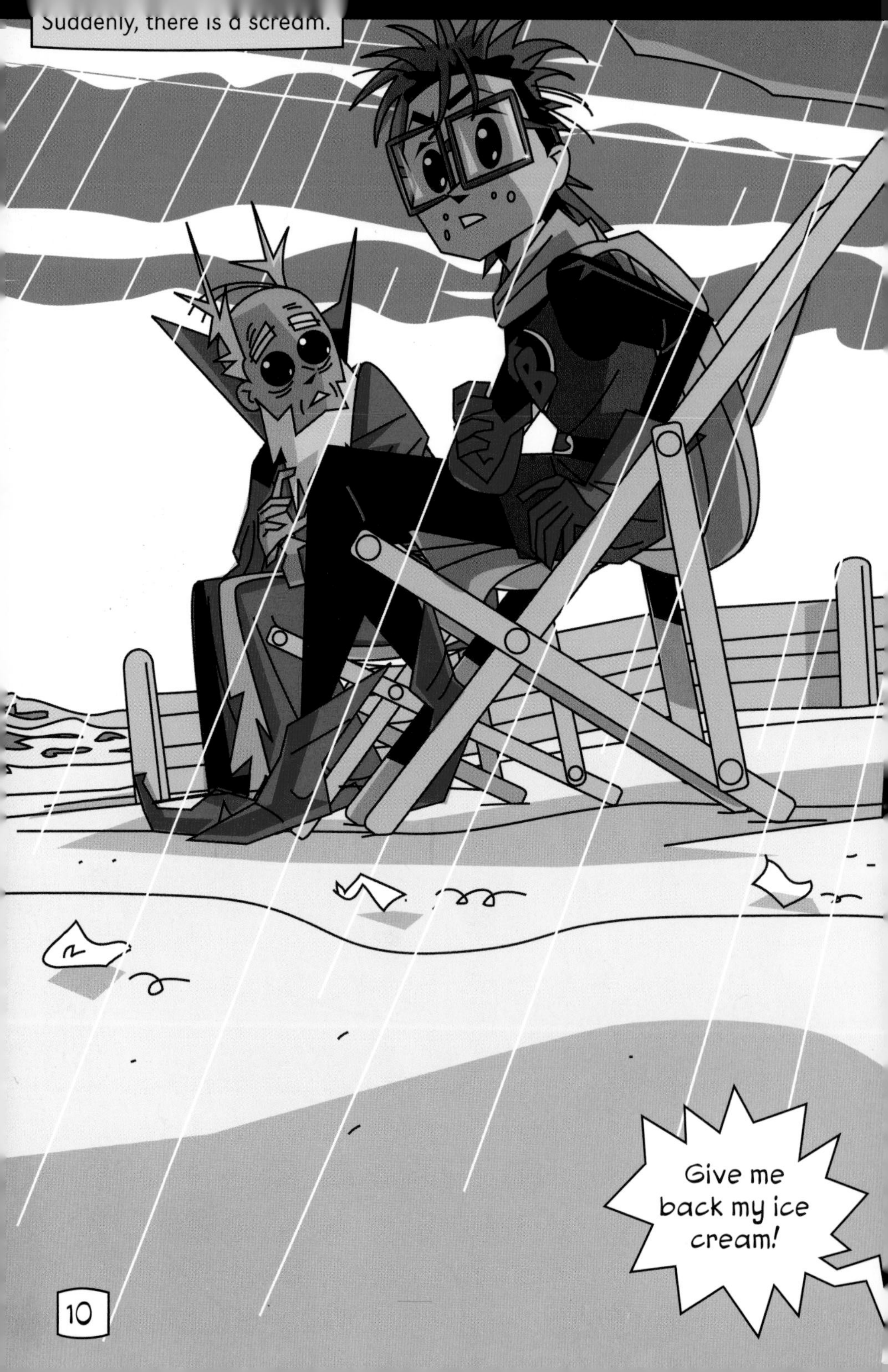
Suddenly, there is a scream.
Give me back my ice cream!

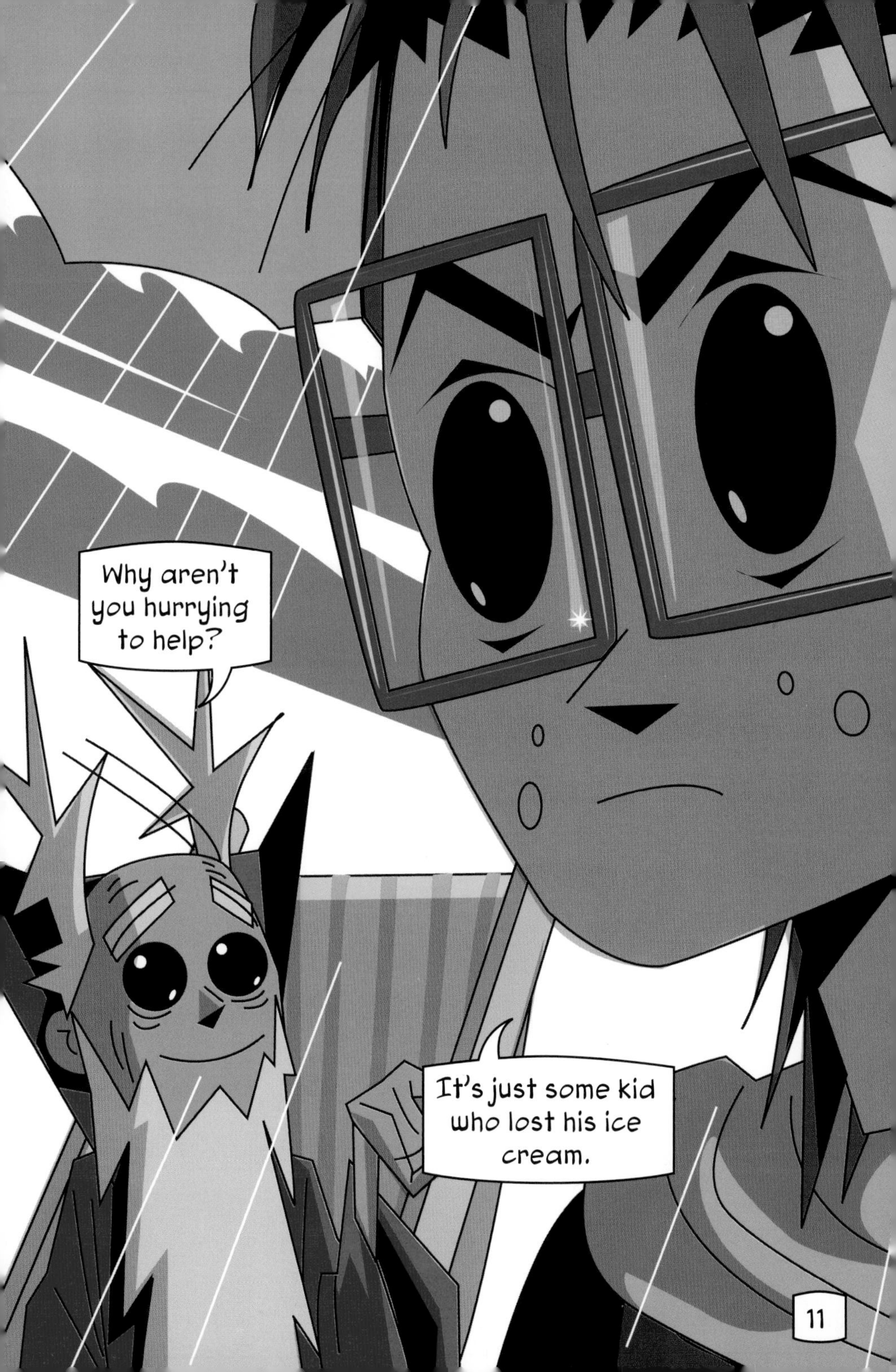
Why aren't you hurrying to help?
It's just some kid who lost his ice cream.

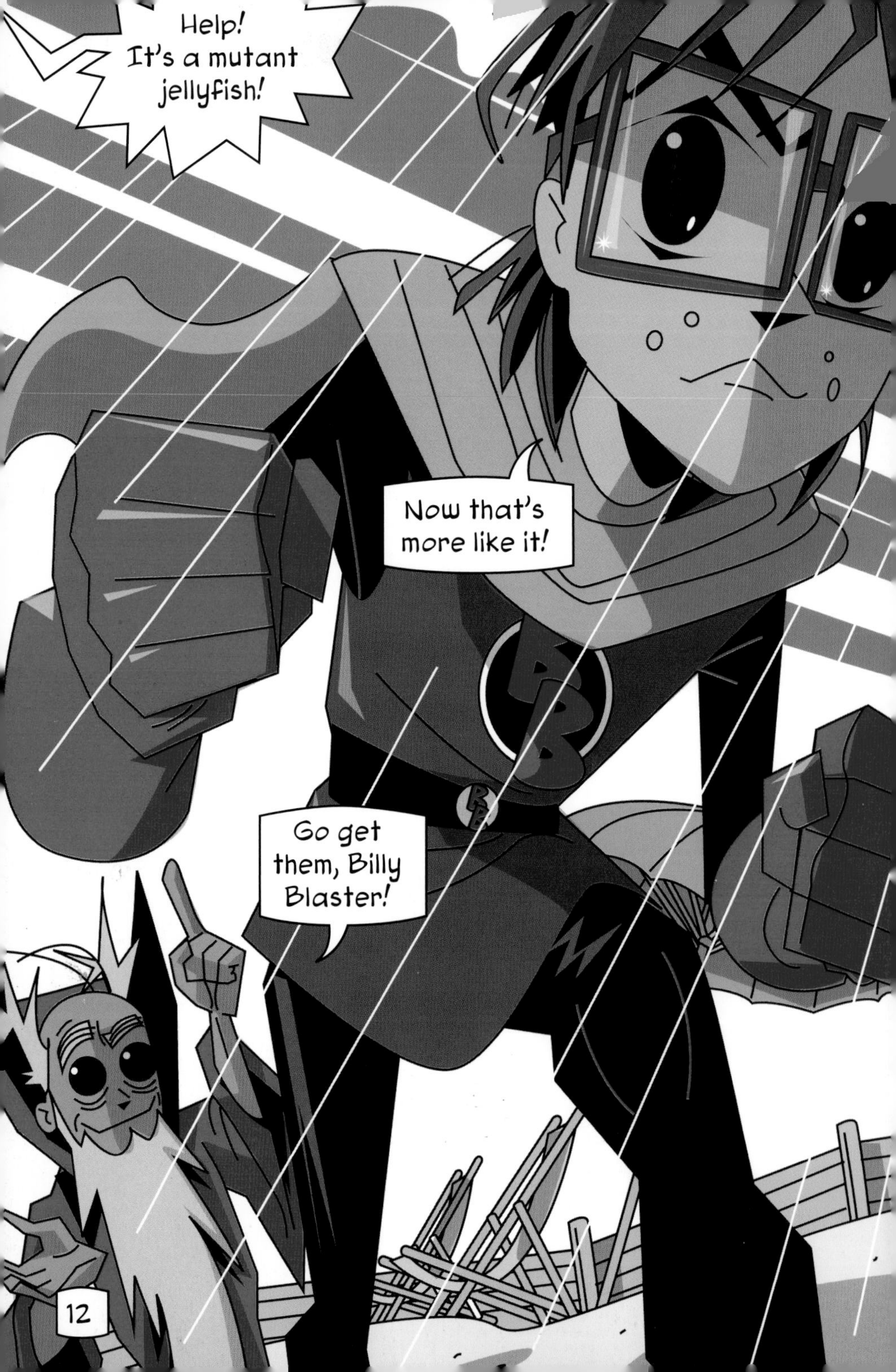
Help! It's a mutant jellyfish!
Now that's more like it!
Go get them, Billy Blaster!

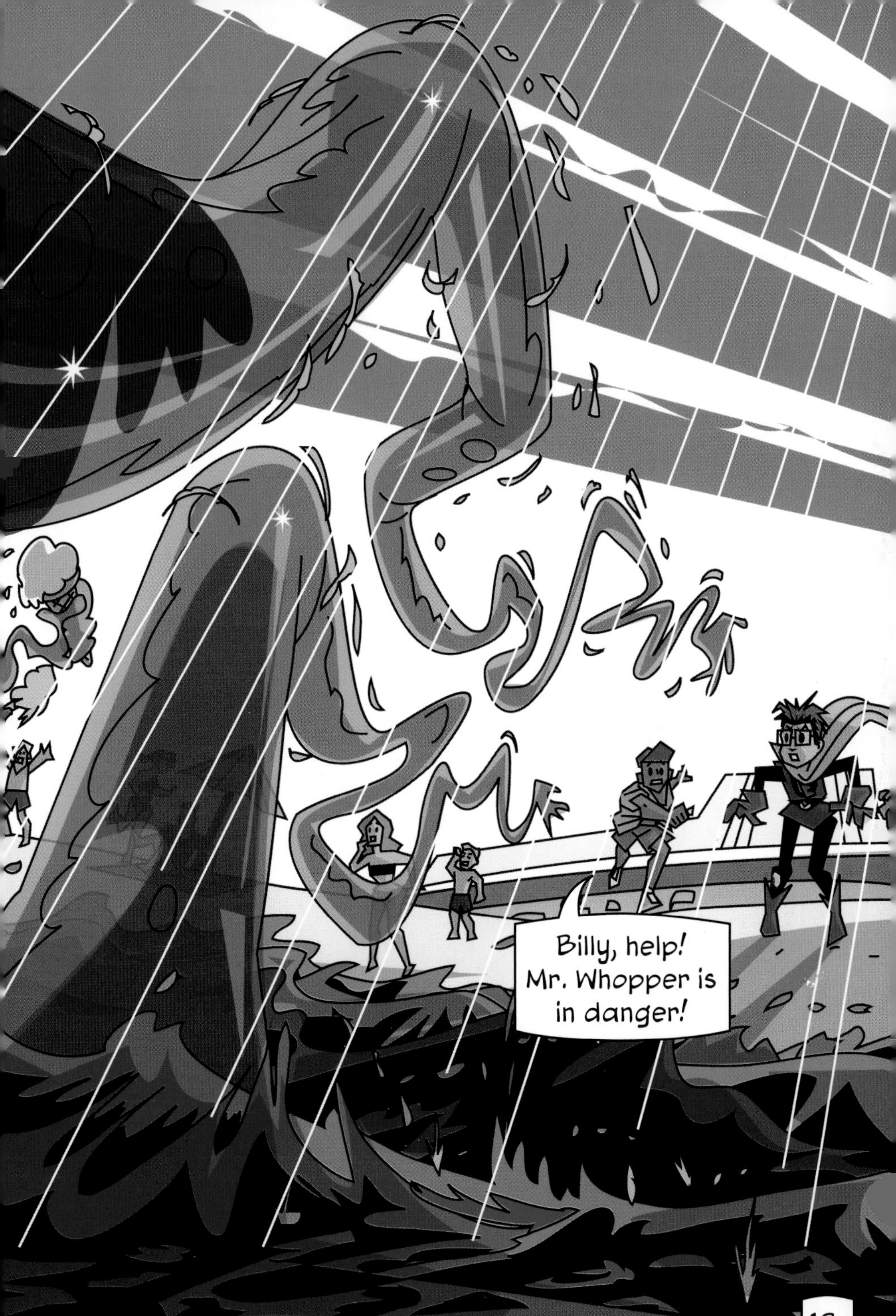
Billy, help! Mr. Whopper is in danger!

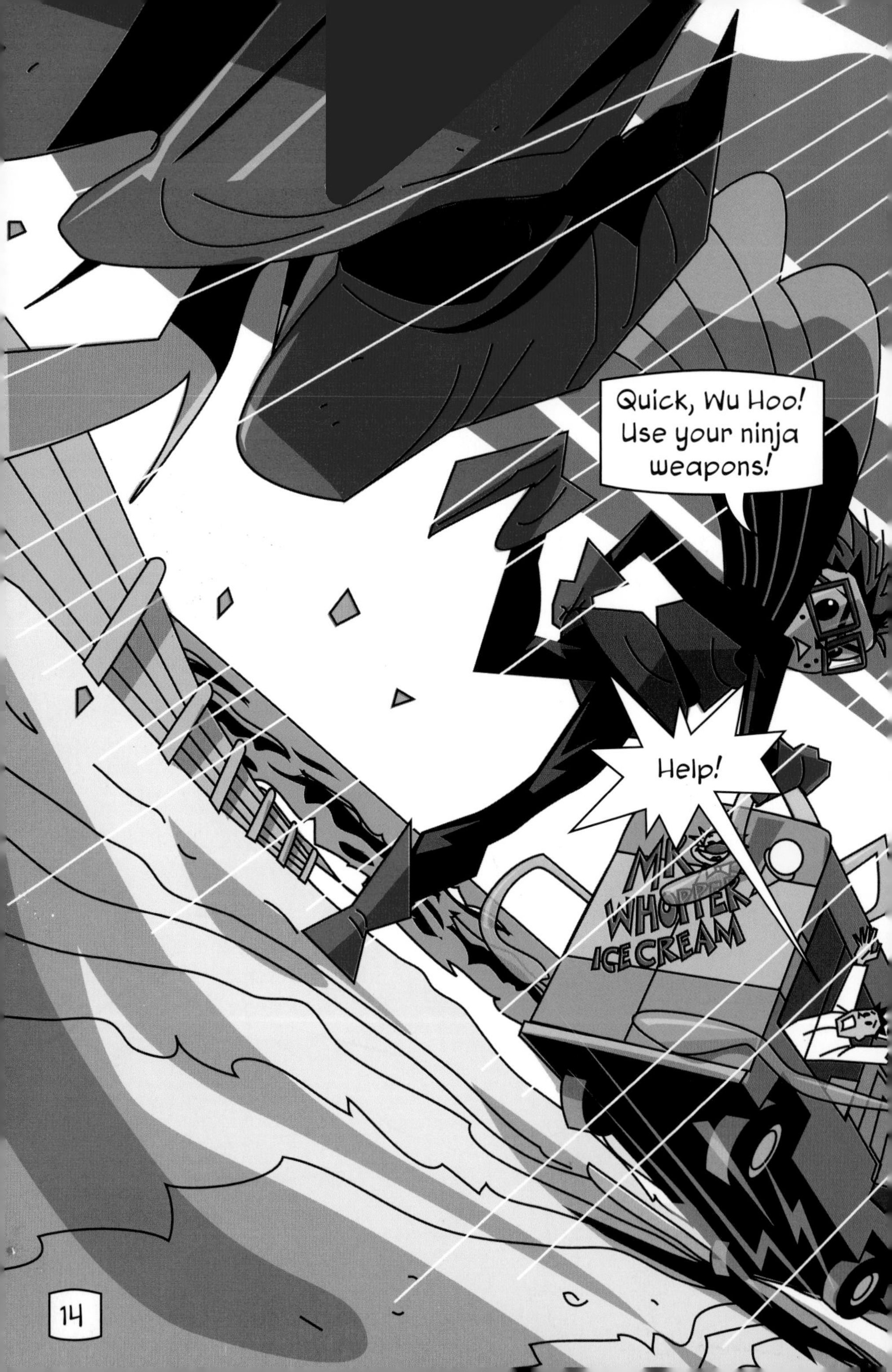
Quick, Wu Hoo! Use your ninja weapons!
Help!
ICE CREAM

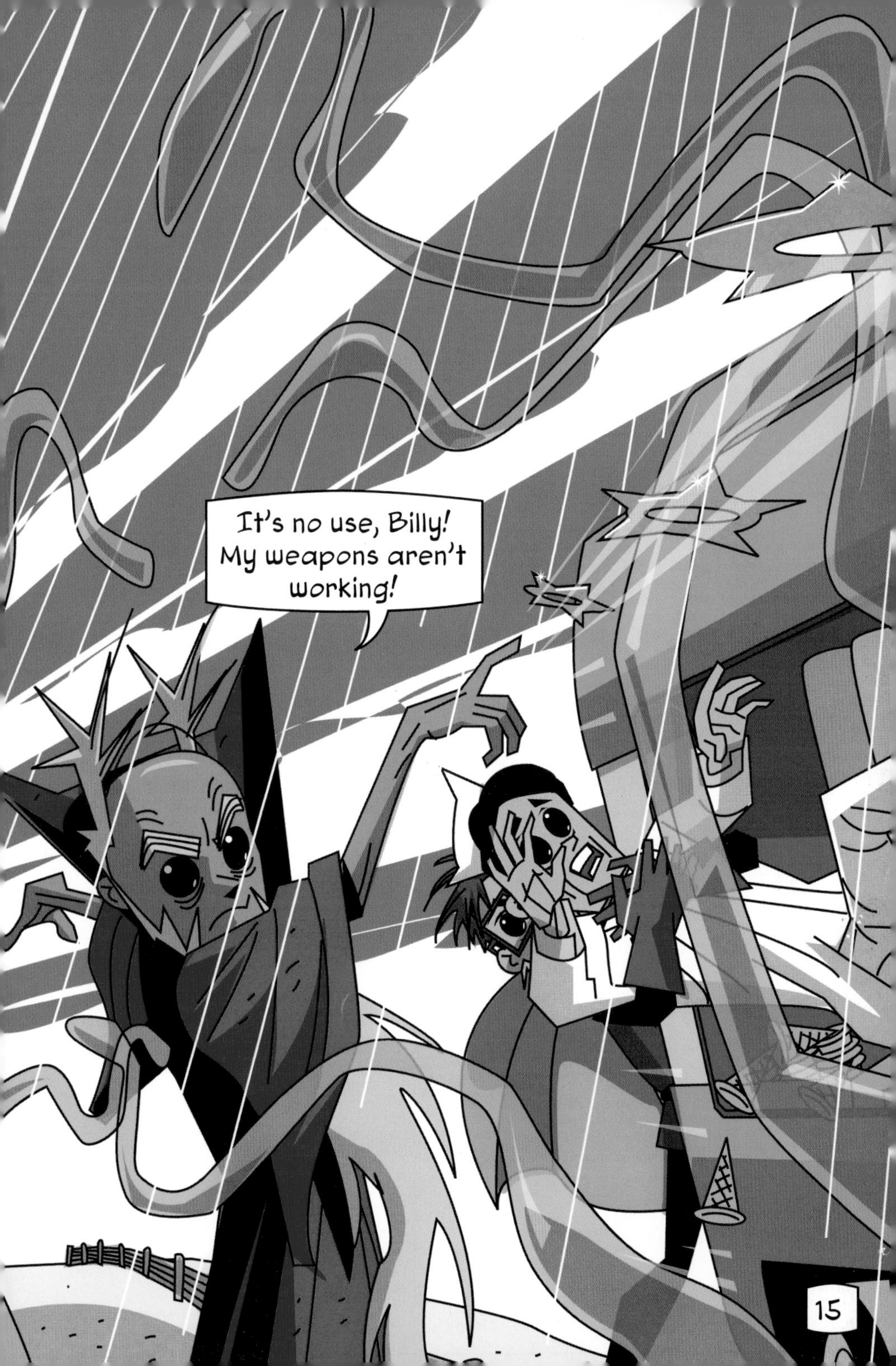
It's no use, Billy! My weapons aren't working!

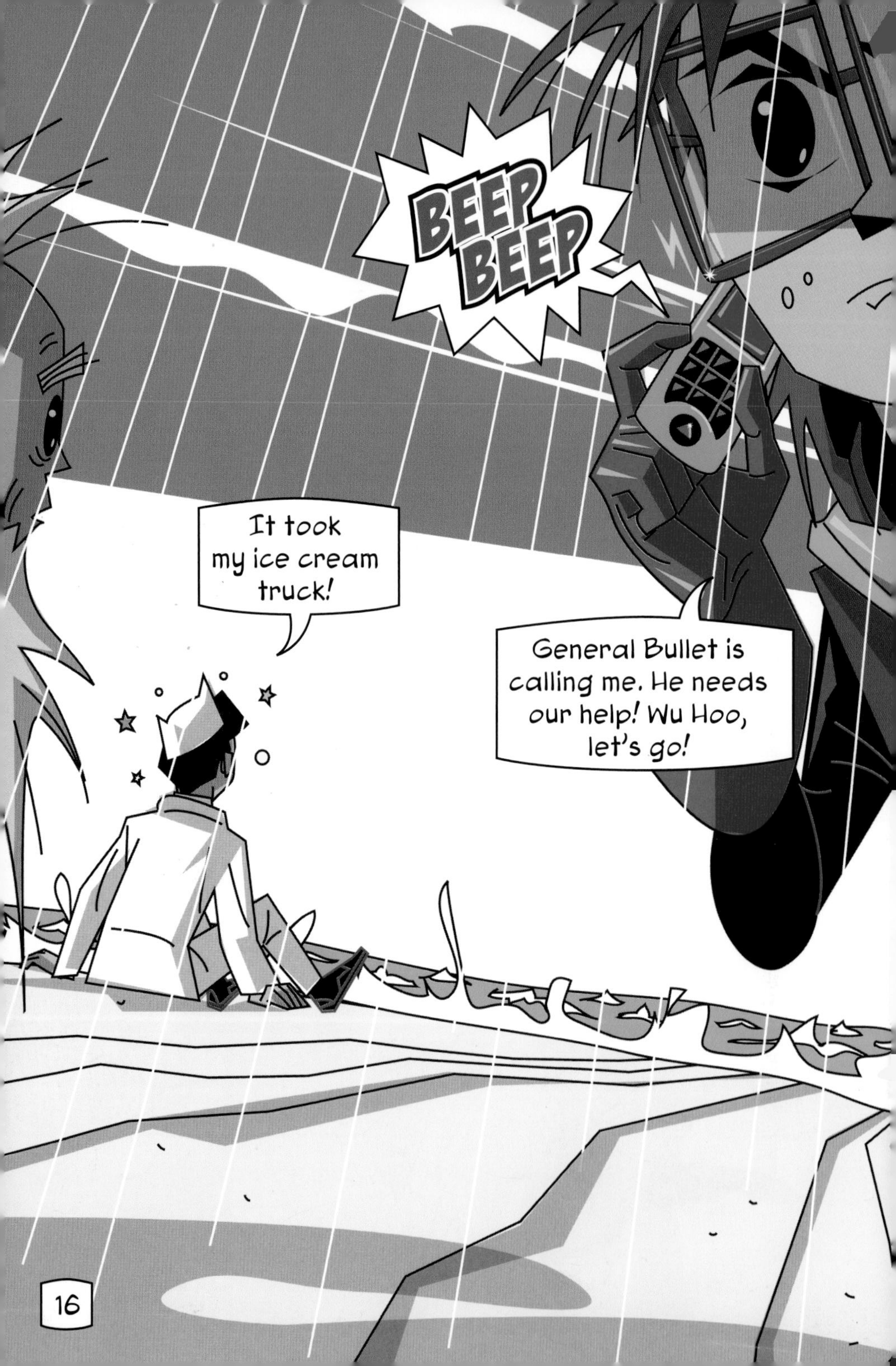
BEEP BEEP
It took my ice cream truck!
General Bullet is calling me. He needs our help! Wu Hoo, let's go!

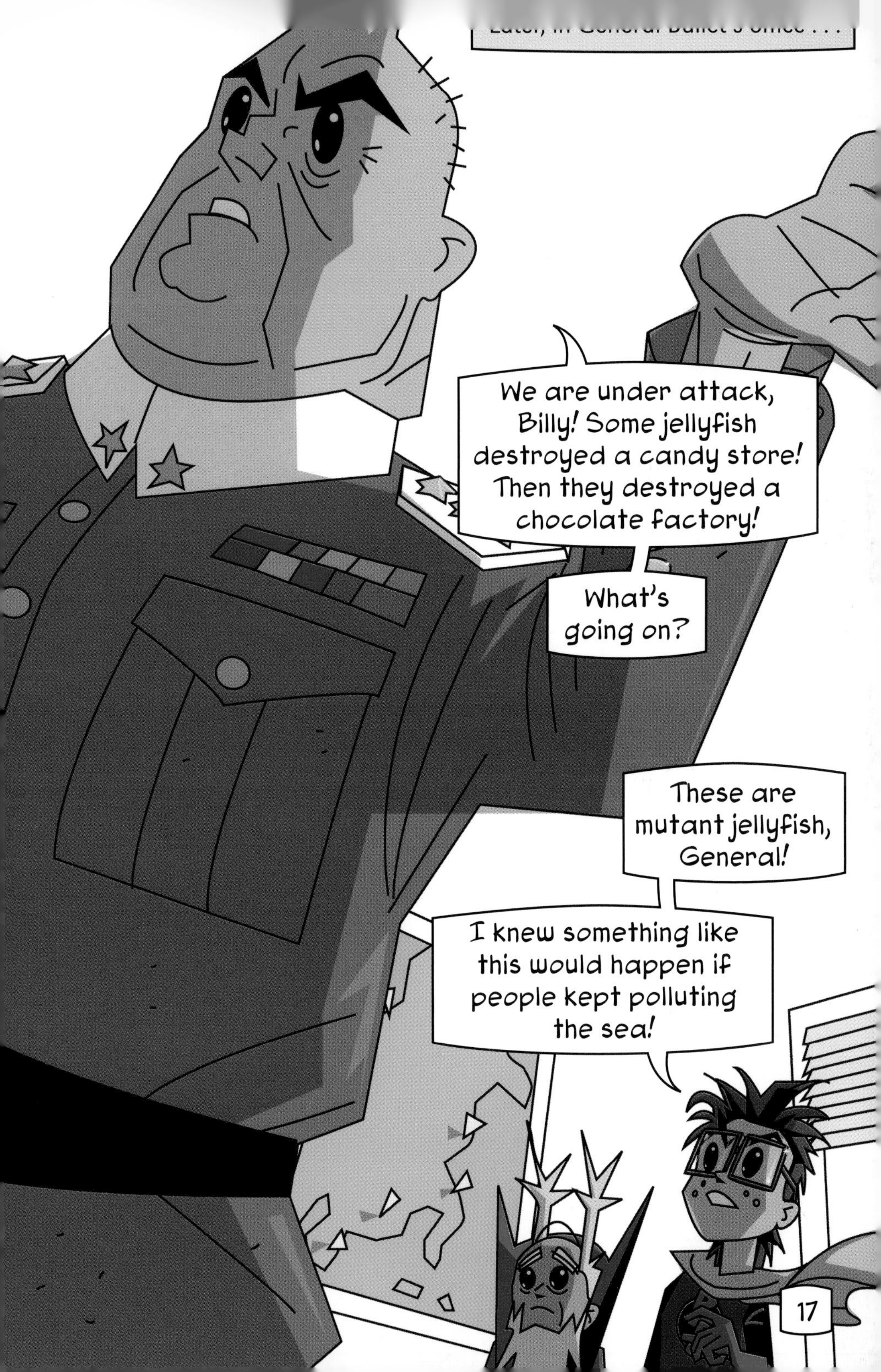

We are under attack, Billy! Some jellyfish destroyed a candy store! Then they destroyed a chocolate factory!
What's going on?
These are mutant jellyfish, General!
I knew something like this would happen if people kept polluting the sea!

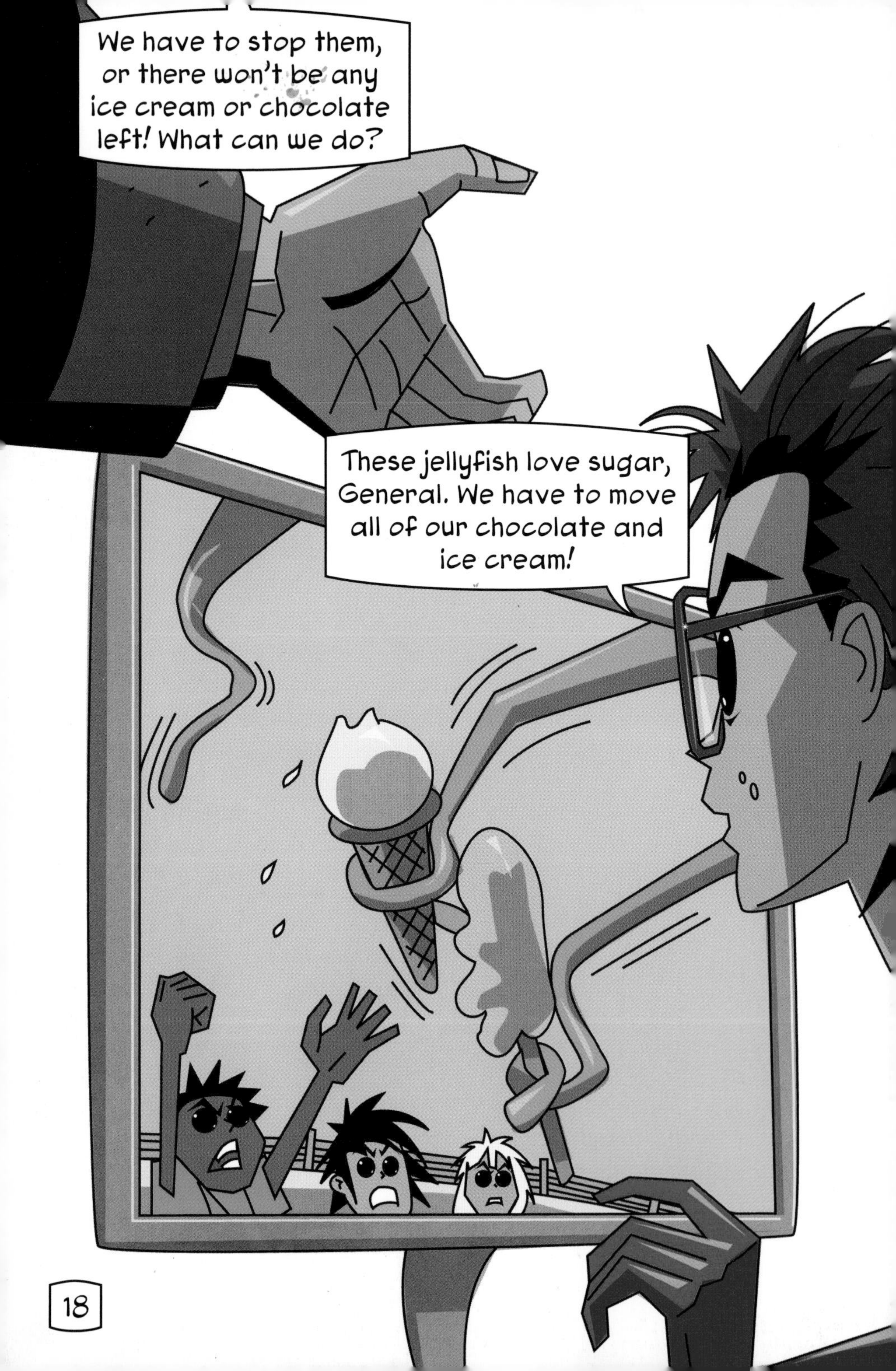
We have to stop them, or there won't be any ice cream or chocolate left! What can we do?
These jellyfish love sugar, General. We have to move all of our chocolate and ice cream!

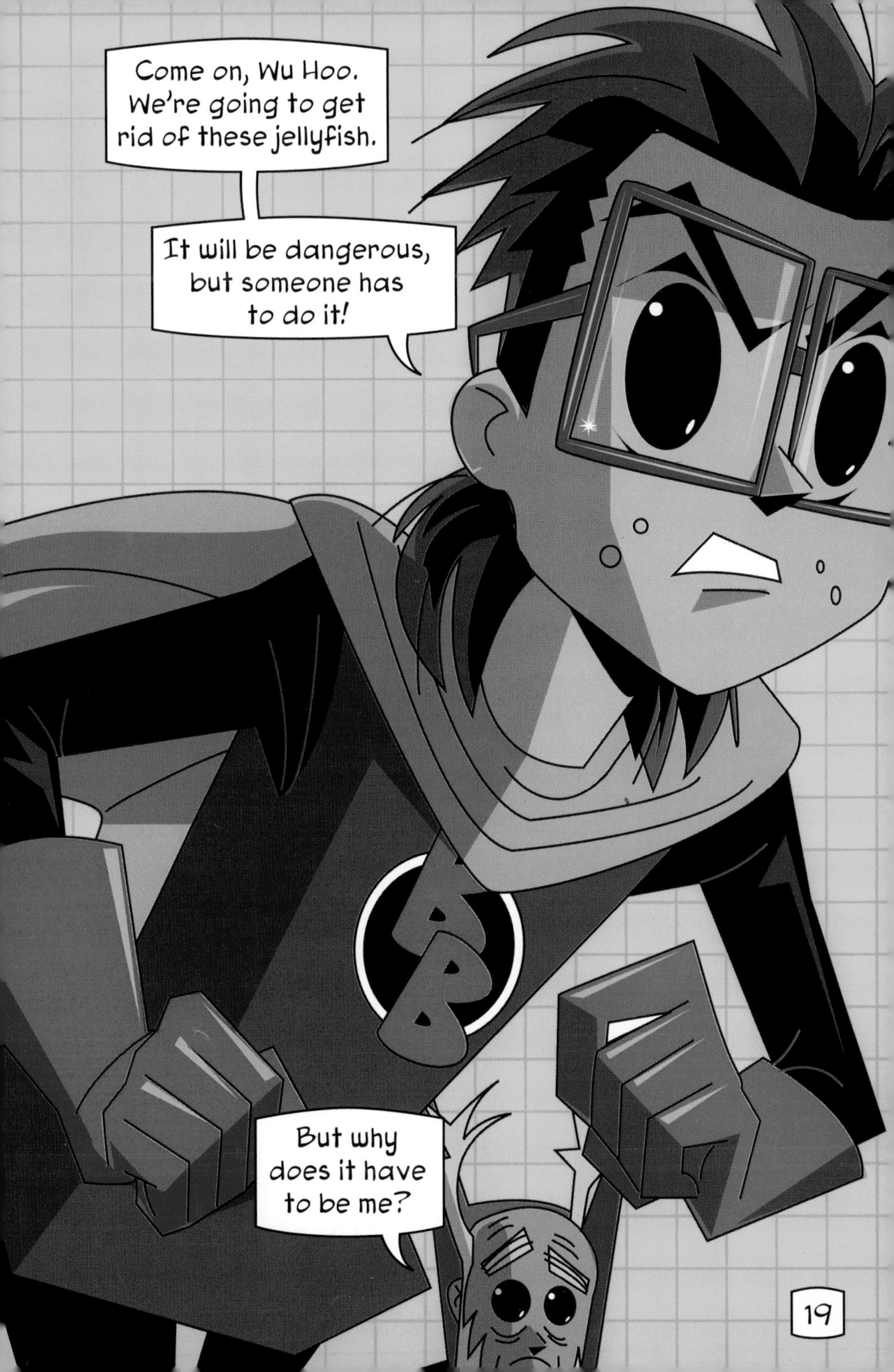
Come on, Wu Hoo. We're going to get rid of these jellyfish.
It will be dangerous, but someone has to do it!
But why does it have to be me?

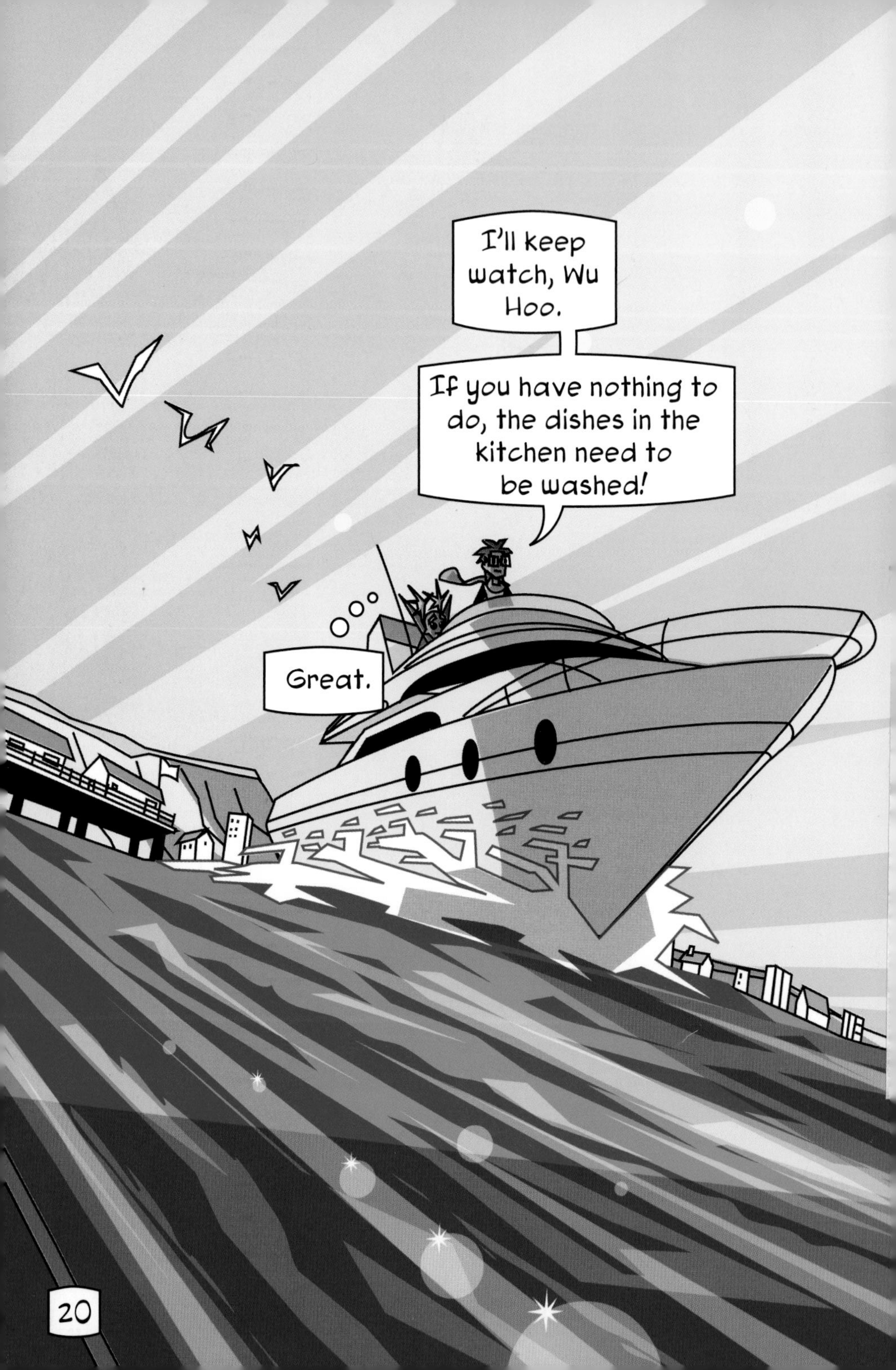
I'll keep watch, Wu Hoo.
If you have nothing to do, the dishes in the kitchen need to be washed!
Great.

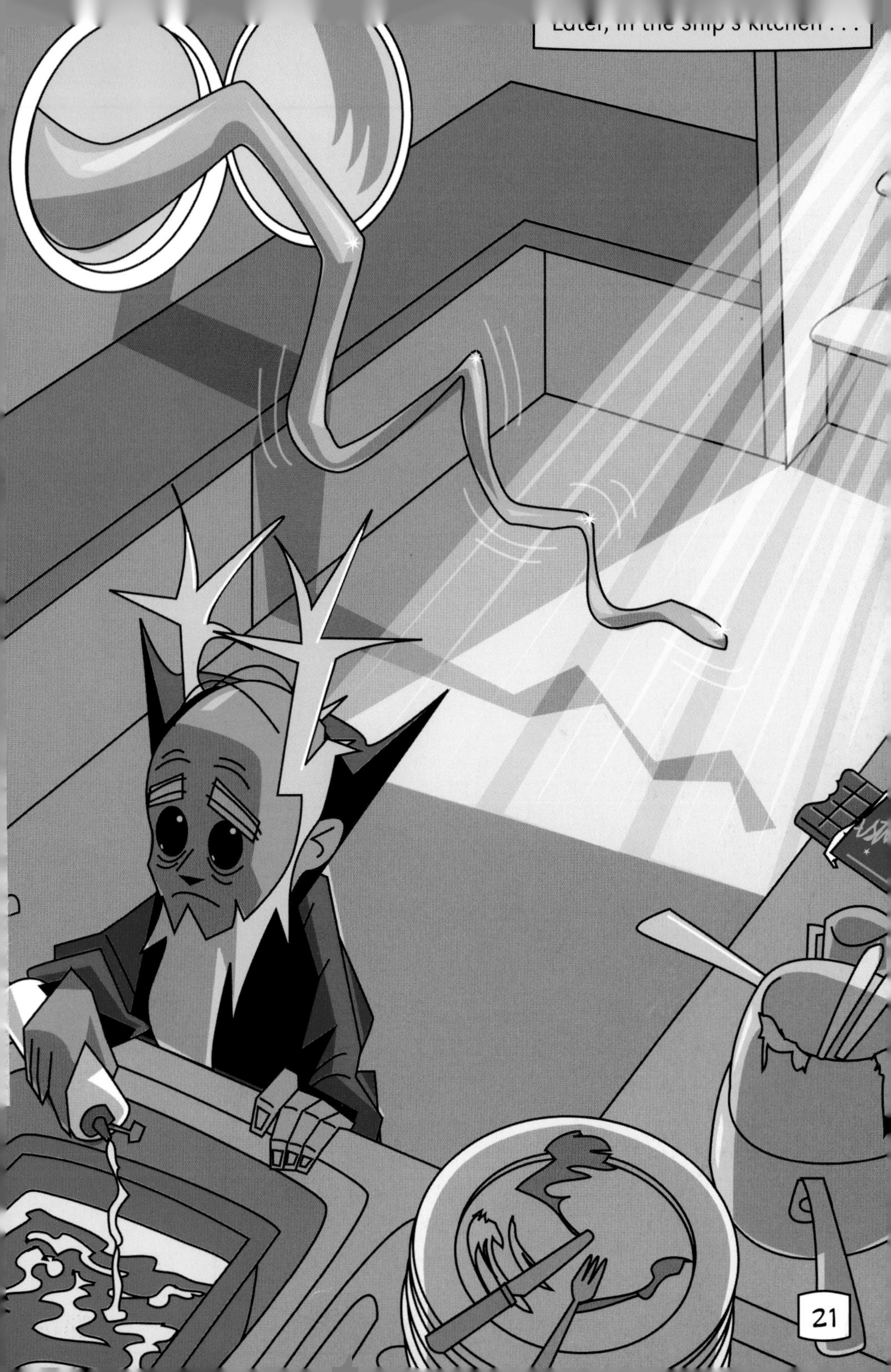
Later, in the ship's kitchen . . .

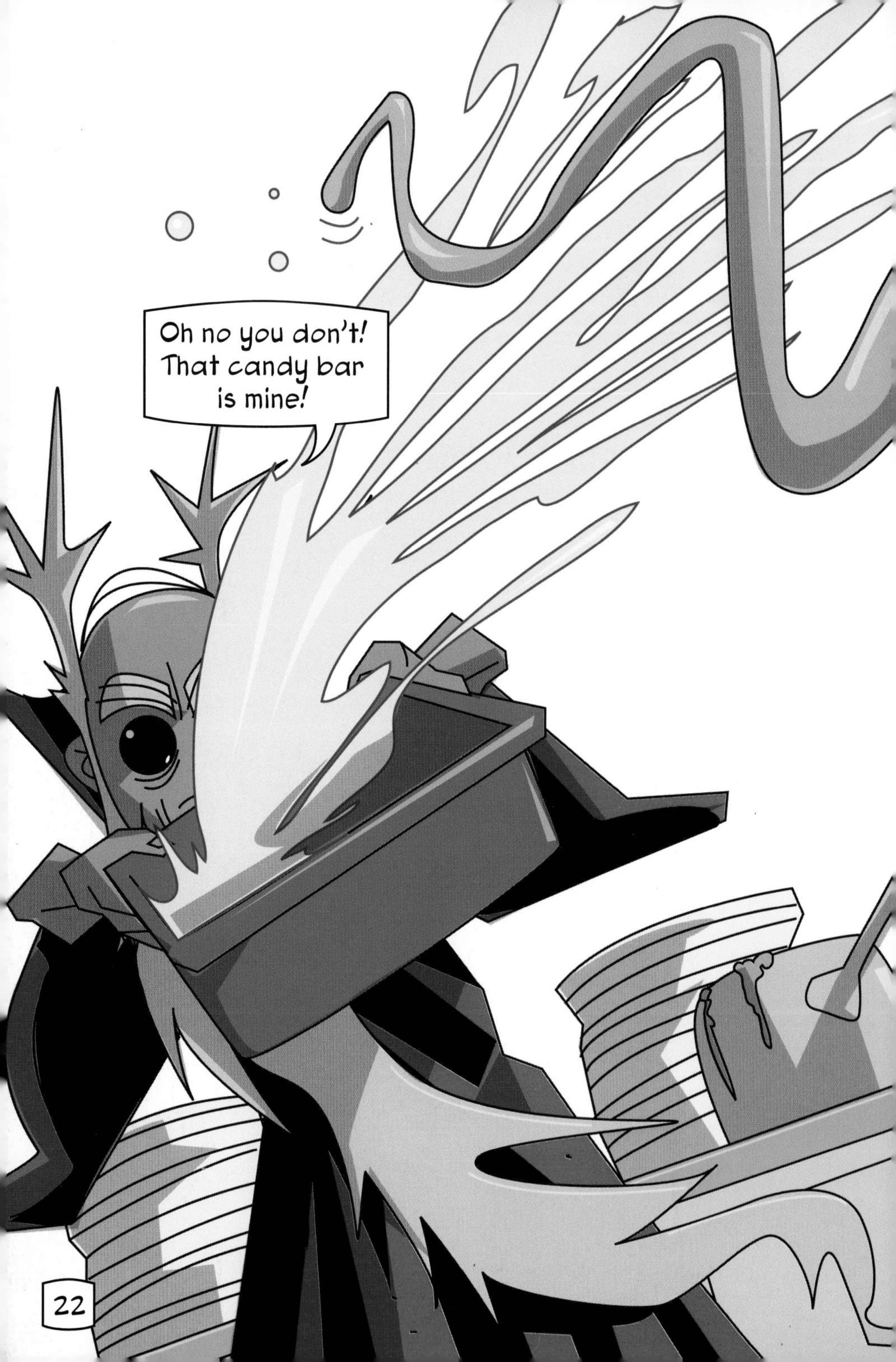
Oh no you don't! That candy bar is mine!

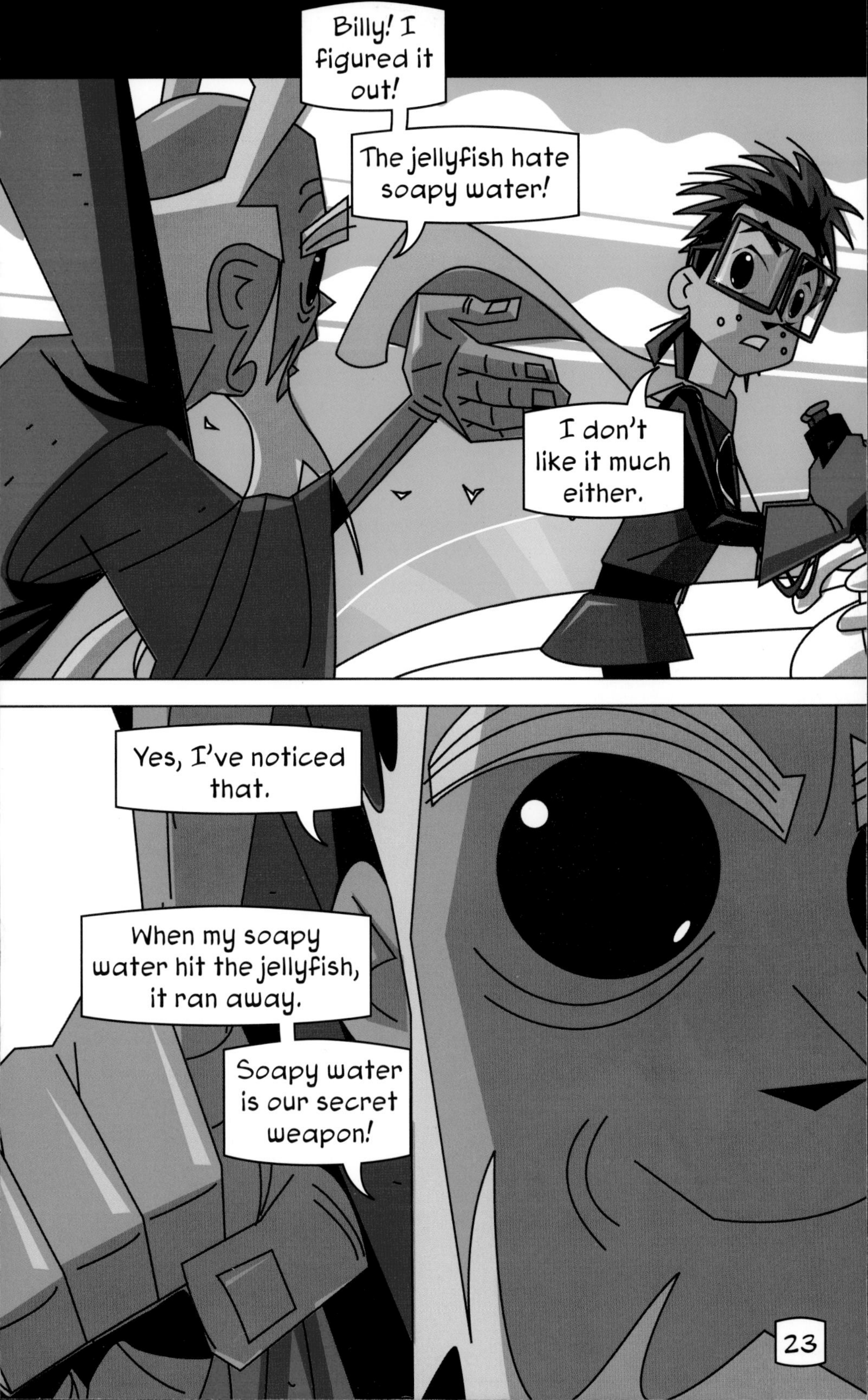
Billy! I figured it out!
The jellyfish hate soapy water!
I don't like it much either.
Yes, I've noticed that.
When my soapy water hit the jellyfish, it ran away.
Soapy water is our secret weapon!

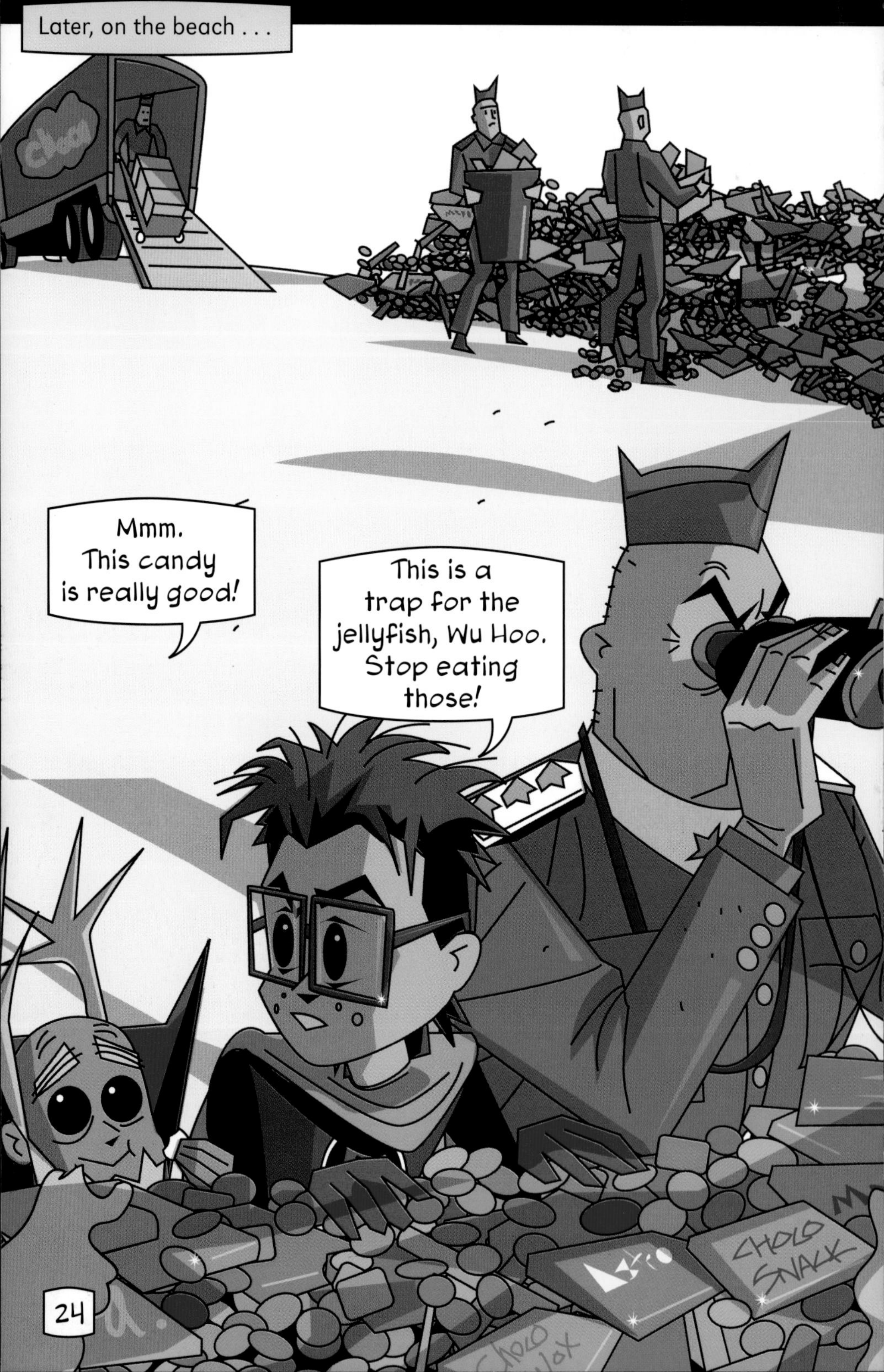
Later, on the beach . . .
Mmm. This candy is really good!
This is a trap for the jellyfish, Wu Hoo. Stop eating those!
CHOLO SNACK

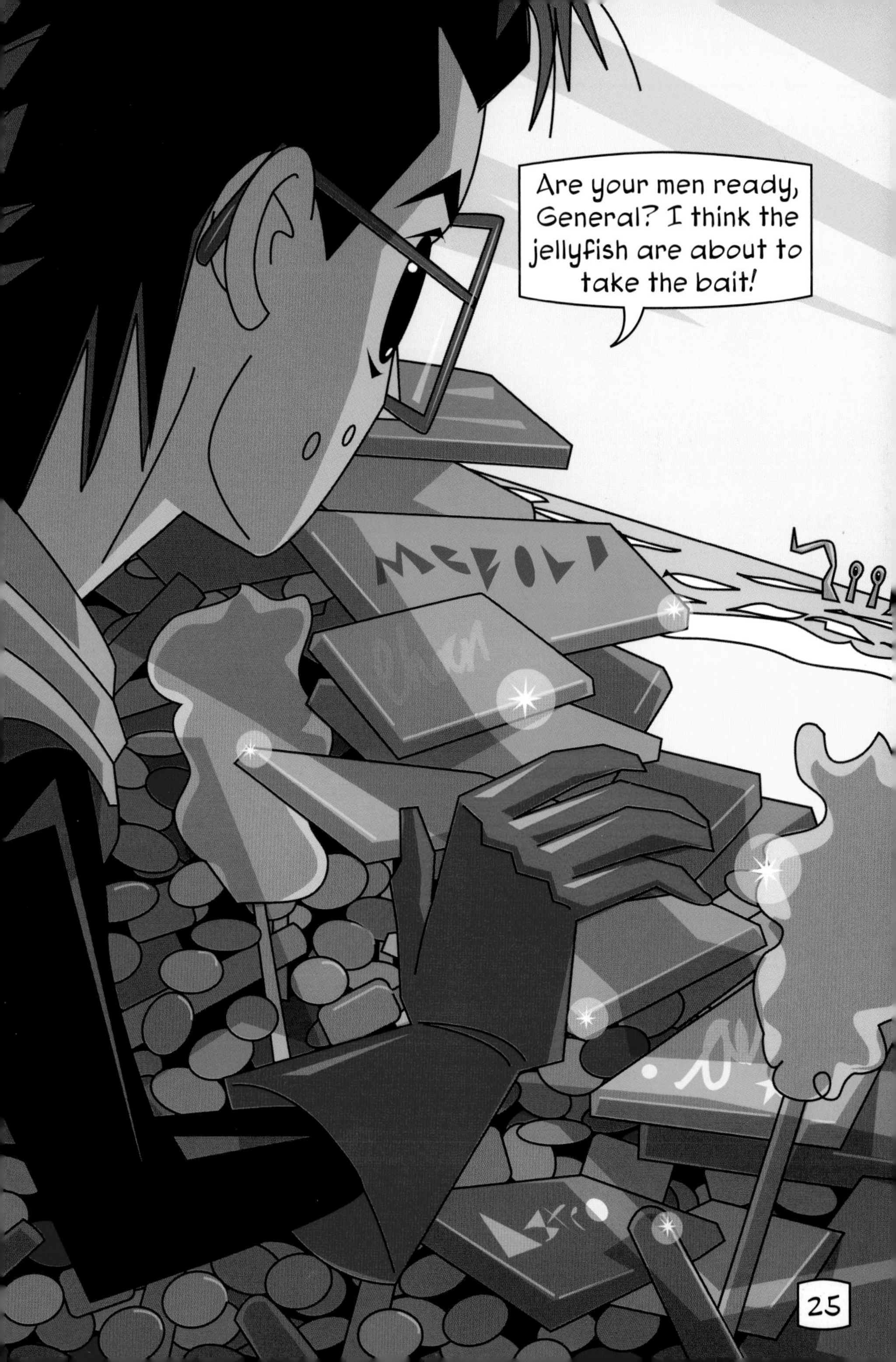
Are your men ready, General? I think the jellyfish are about to take the bait!

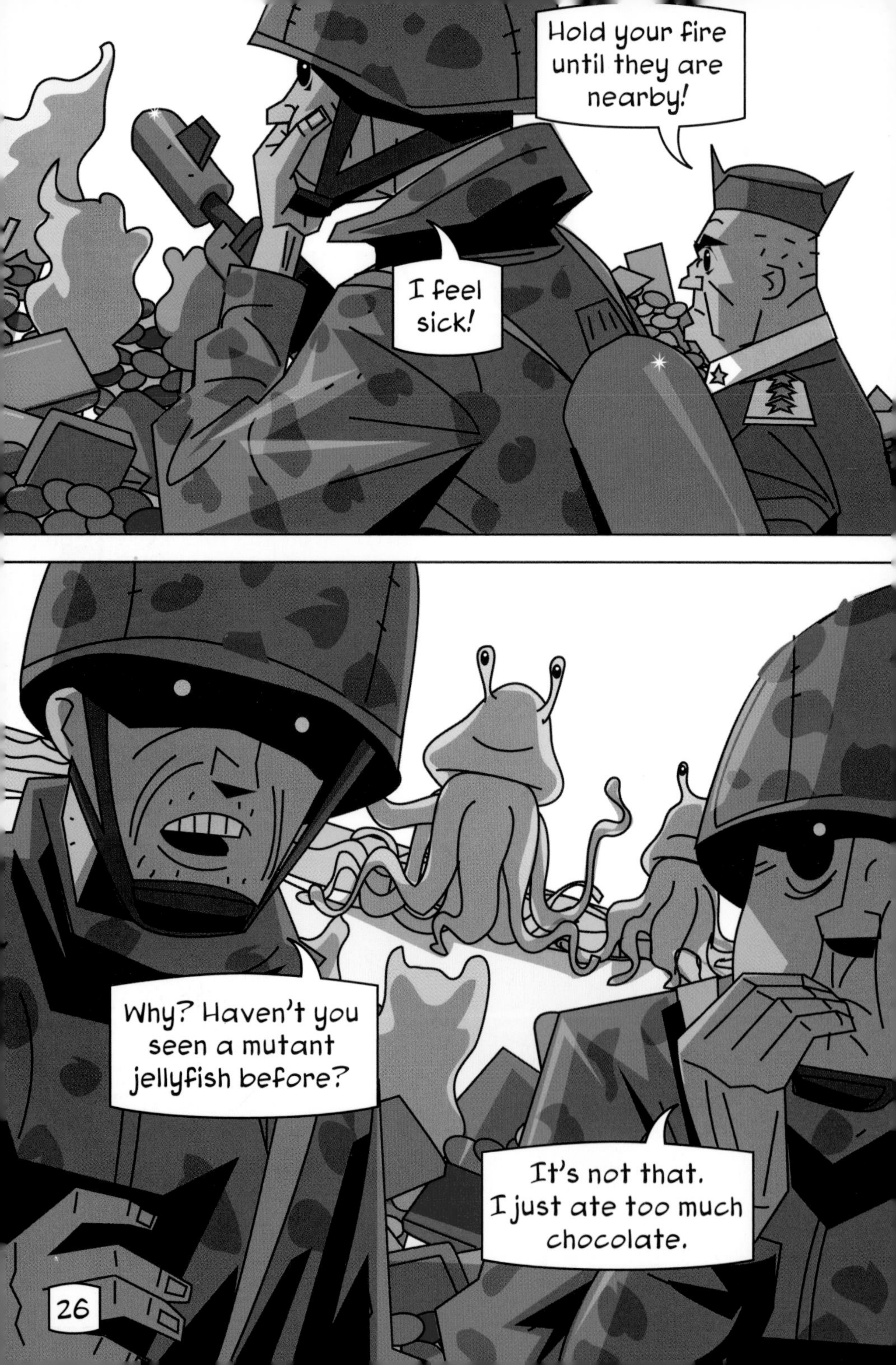
Hold your fire until they are nearby!
I feel sick!
Why? Haven't you seen a mutant jellyfish before?
It's not that. I just ate too much chocolate.

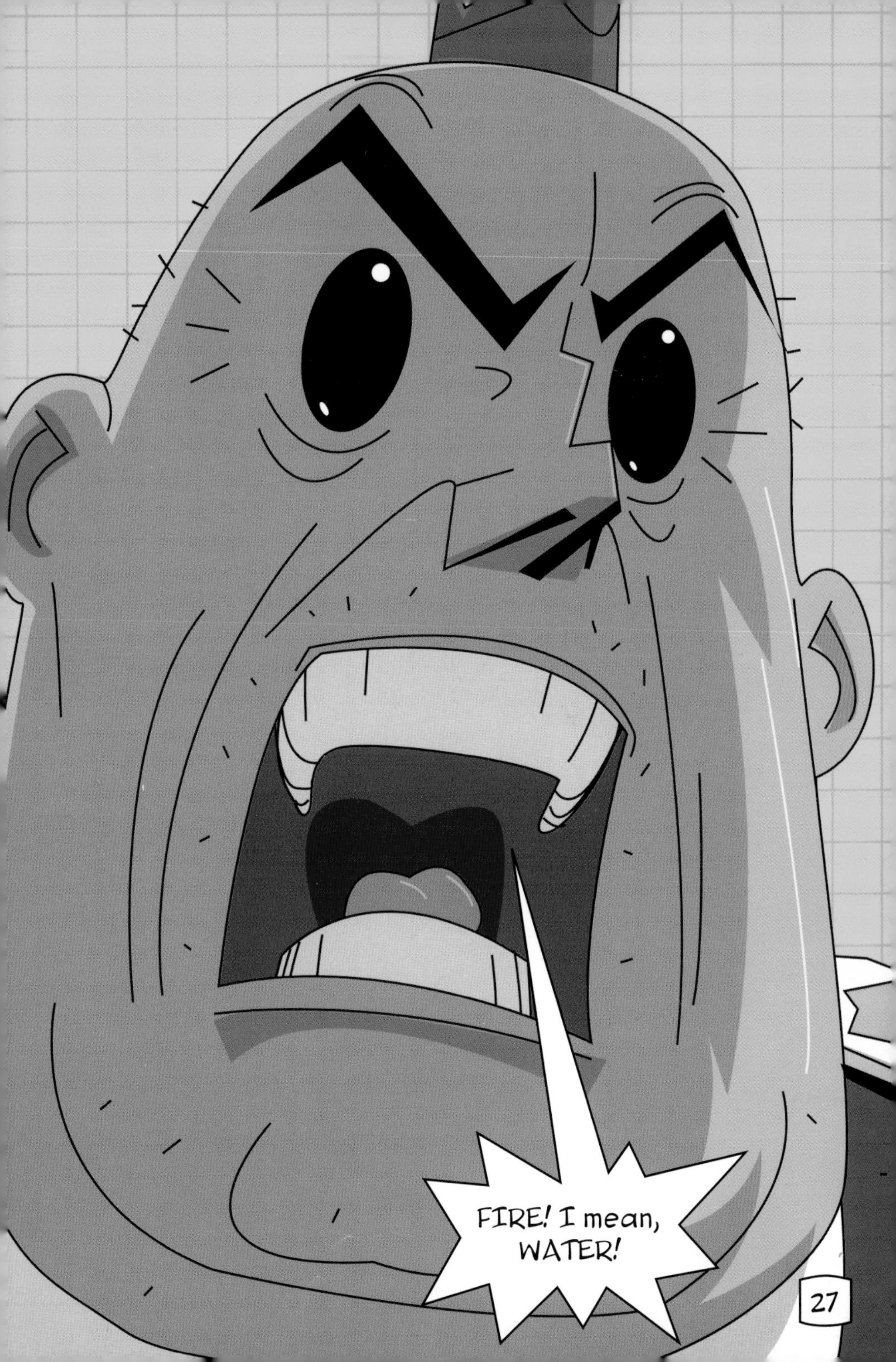
FIRE! I mean, WATER!

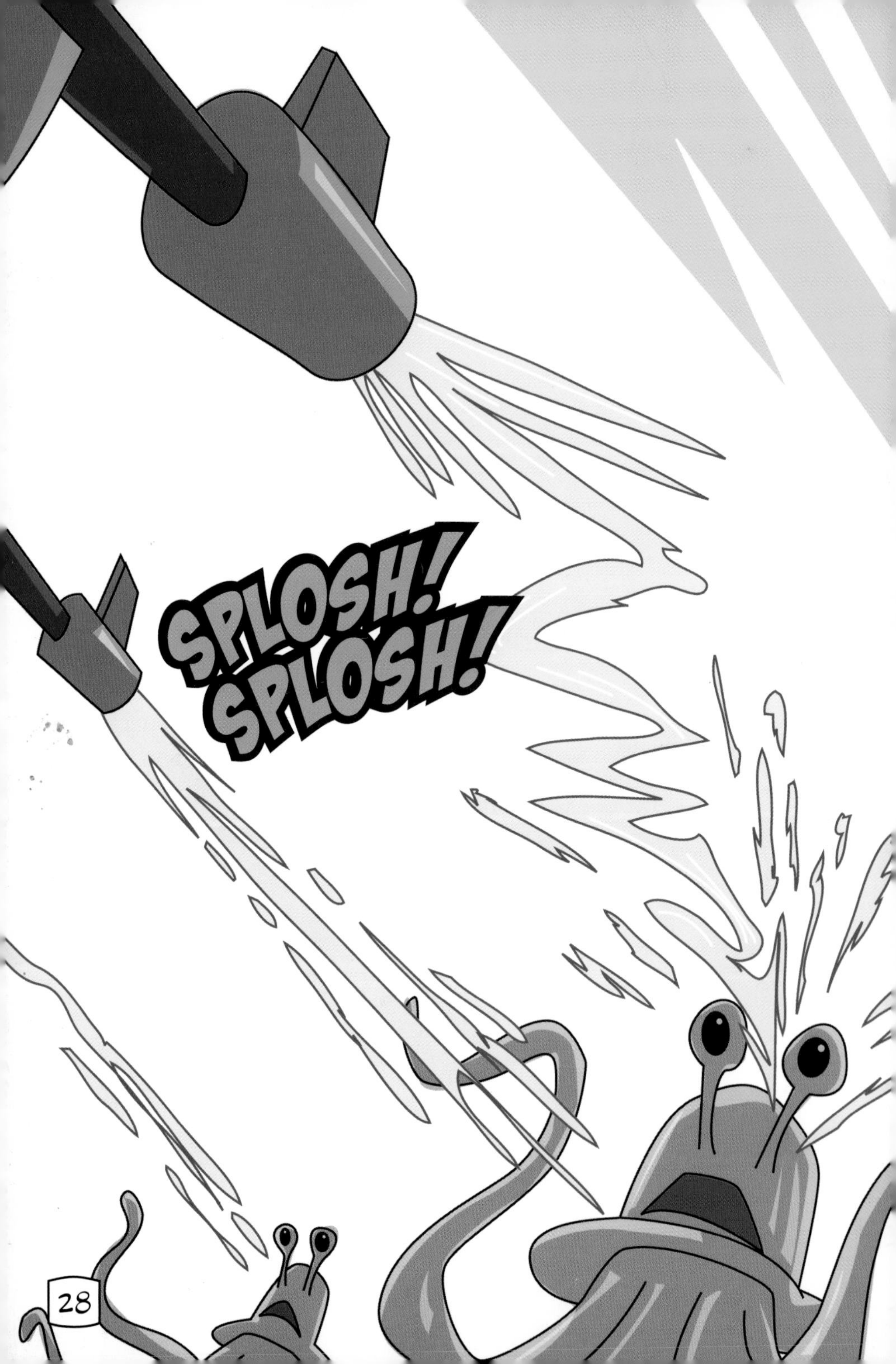
SPLOSH! SPLOSH!

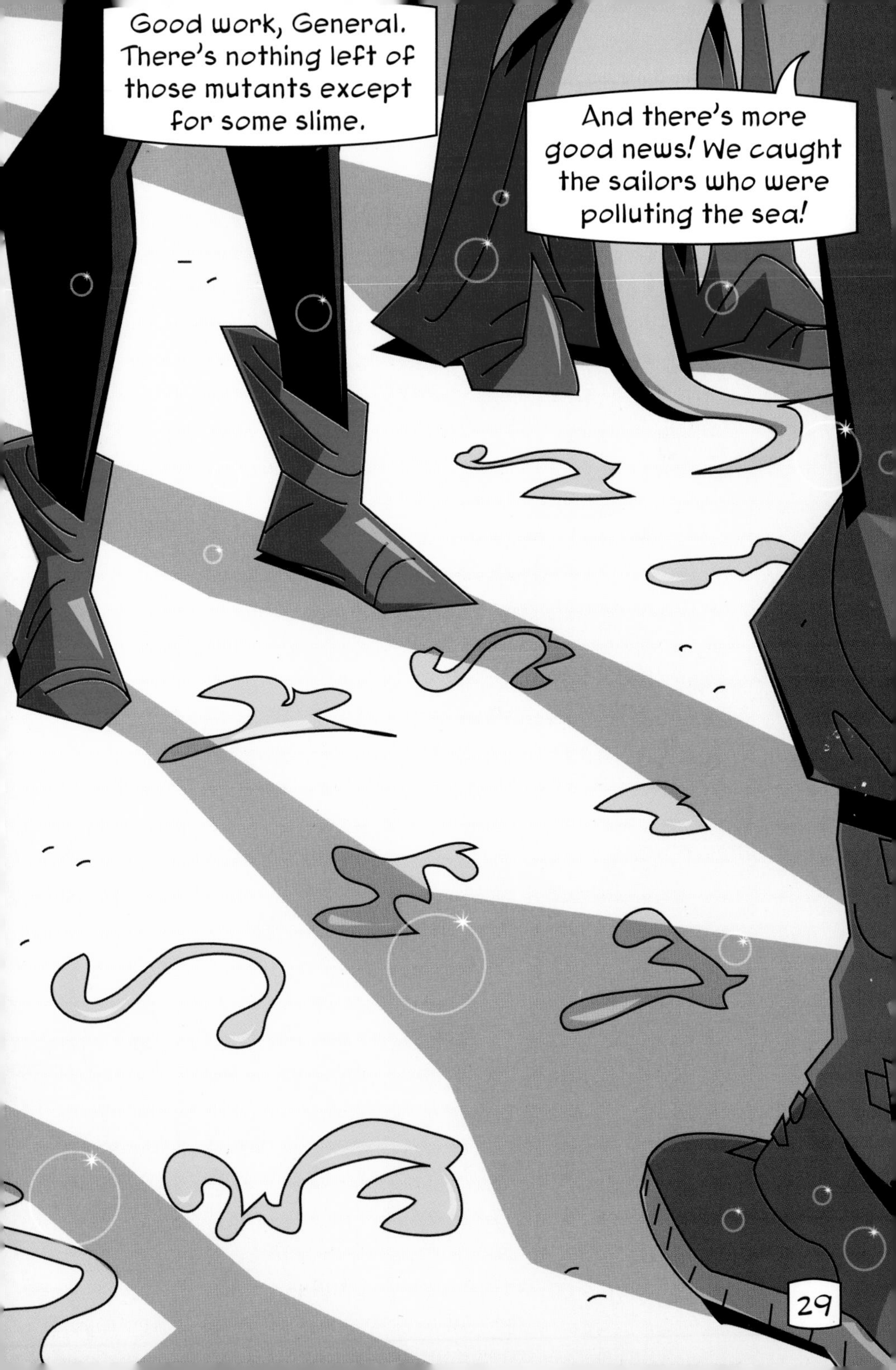
Good work, General. There's nothing left of those mutants except for some slime.
And there's more good news! We caught the sailors who were polluting the sea!

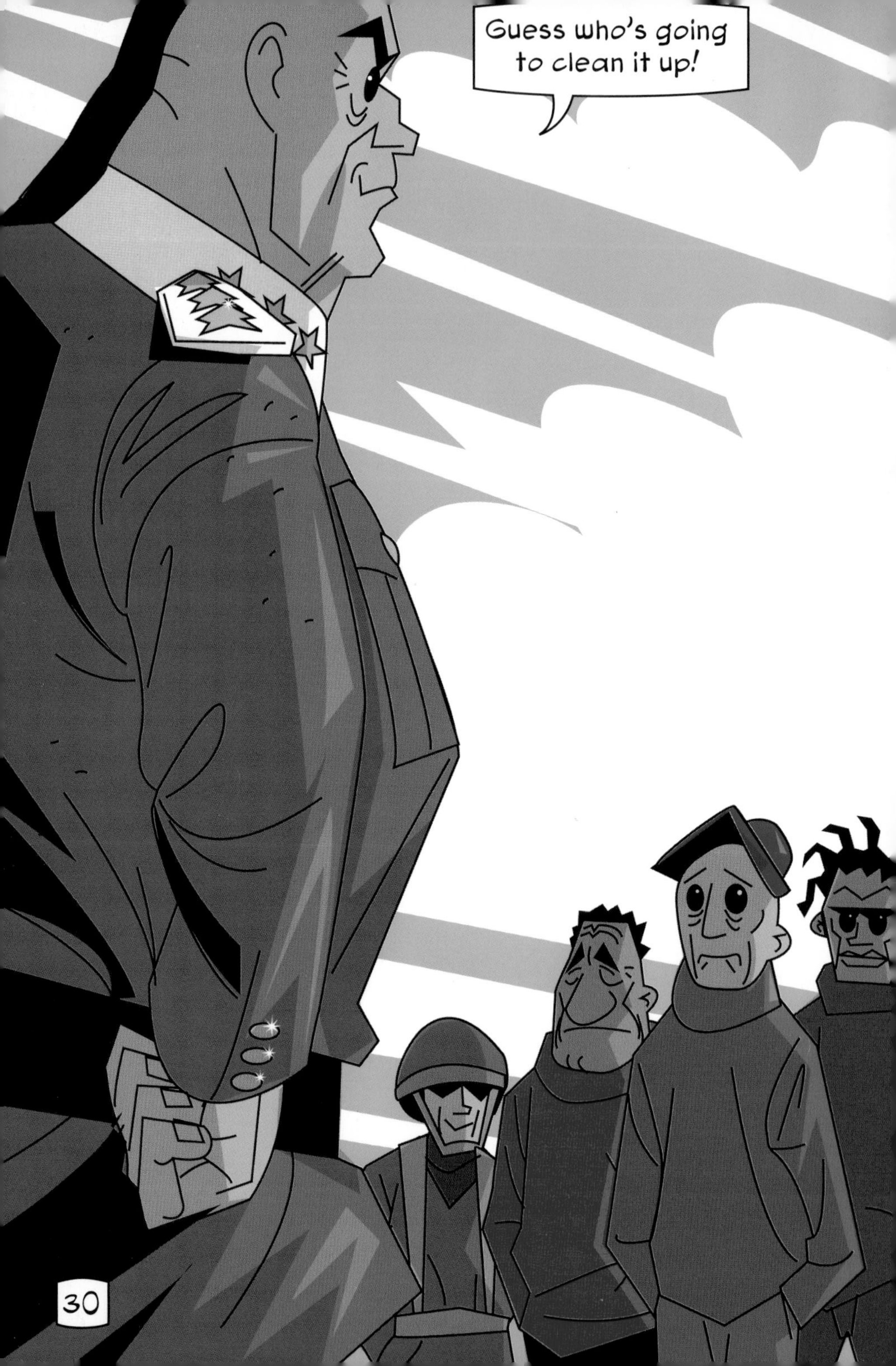
Guess who's going to clean it up!

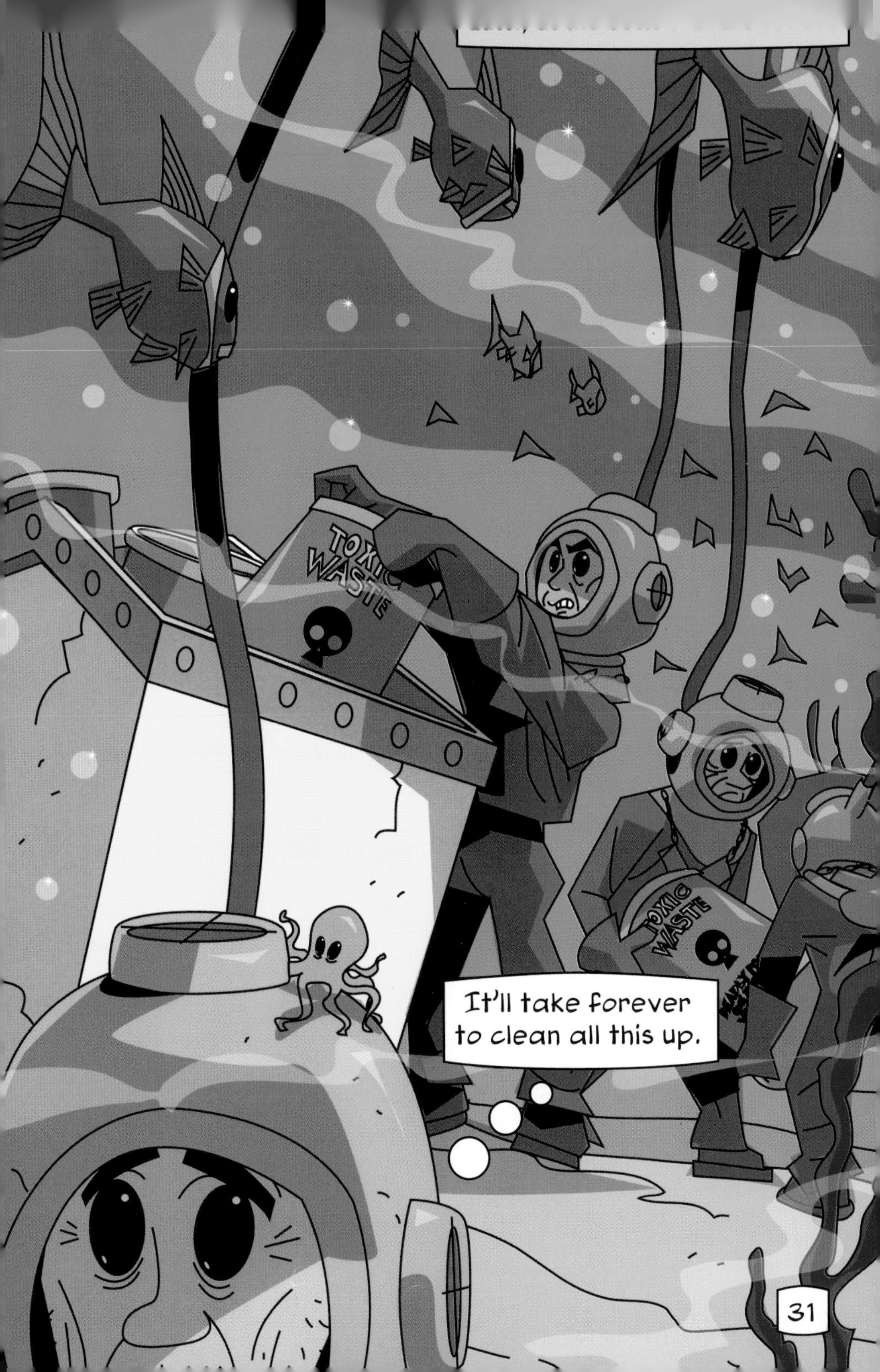
TOXIC WASTE
It'll take forever to clean all this up.
TOXIC WASTE

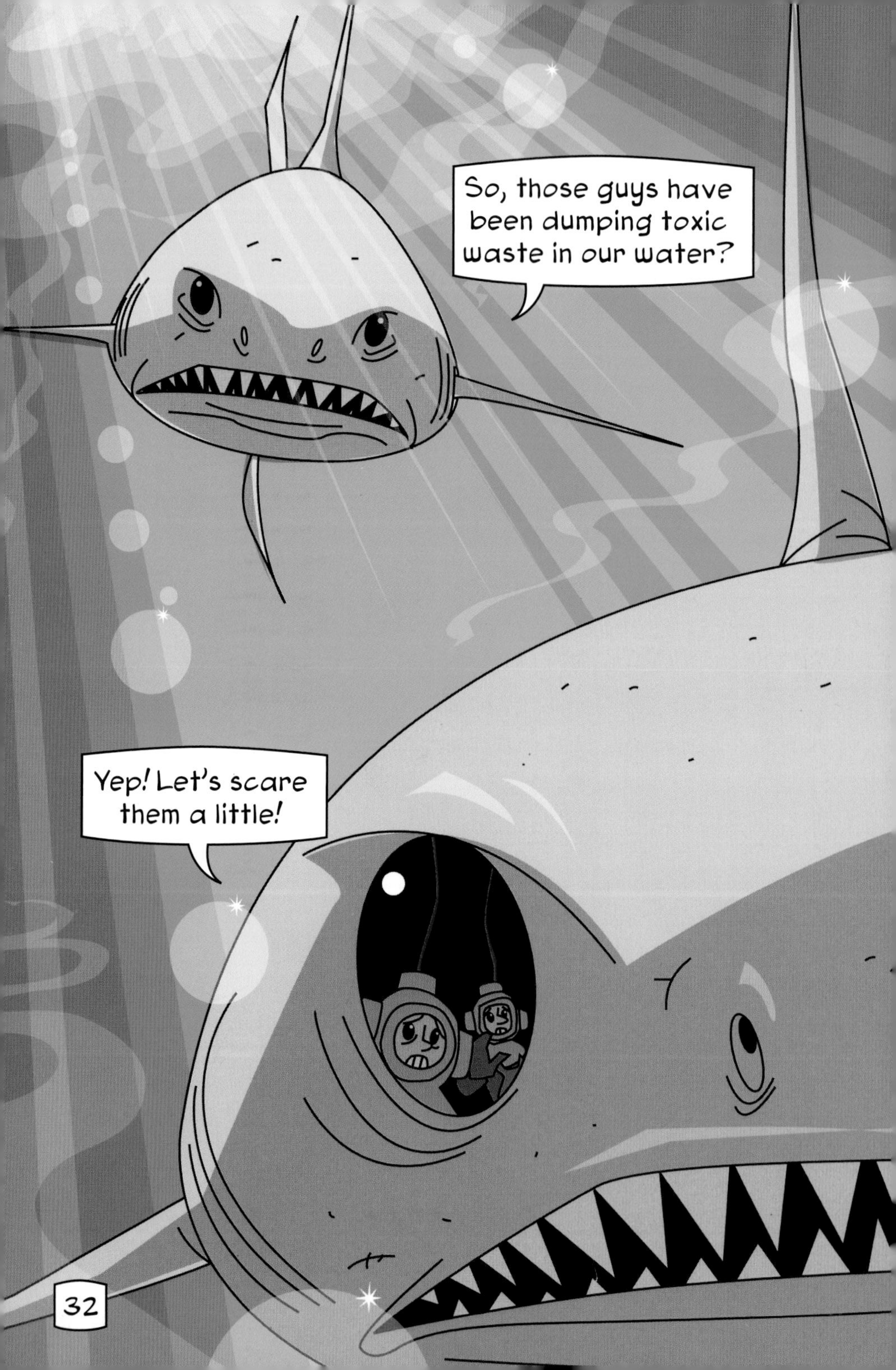
So, those guys have been dumping toxic waste in our water?
Yep! Let's scare them a little!

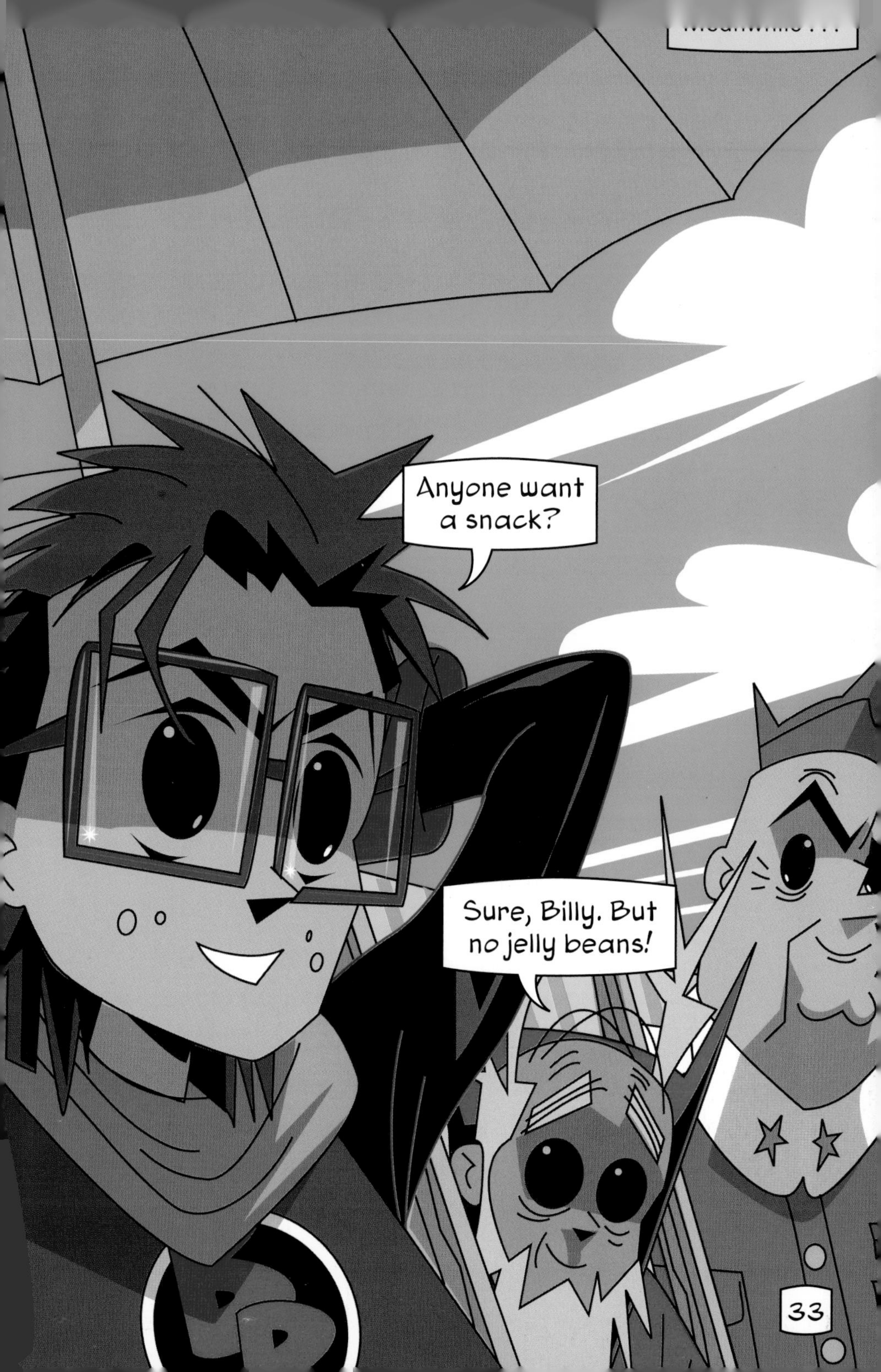
Anyone want a snack?
Sure, Billy. But no jelly beans!

ABOUT THE AUTHOR

David Orme was a teacher for 18 years before he became a full-time writer. When he is not writing books, he travels around the country, giving performances, running writing workshops, and running courses. David has written more than 250 books, including poetry collections and anthologies, fiction and nonfiction, and school text books. He lives in Winchester, England.

ABOUT THE ILLUSTRATOR

Peter Richardson's illustrations have appeared in a variety of productions and publications. He has done character designs and storyboards for many of London's top animation studios as well as artwork for advertising campaigns by big companies like BP and British Airways. His work often appears in *The Sunday Times* and *The Guardian*, as well as many magazines. He loves the Billy Blaster books and looks forward to seeing where Billy and his ninja sidekick, Wu Hoo, will end up next.

GLOSSARY

bait (BAYT)—things used in a trap to catch something

dangerous (DAYN-jur-uhss)—something or someone that might cause harm or injury

factory (FAK-tuh-ree)—a building where things are made in large numbers by machines

jellyfish (JEL-ee-fish)—a sea creature with a soft body that jiggles like jelly and has tentacles

mutant (MYOOT-ant)—a living thing that has developed different qualities because of a change in its genes

polluting (puh-LOOT-ing)—making something dirty or unclean

toxic waste (TOK-sik WAYST)—poisonous garbage

sailors (SAY-lurz)—people in a ship's crew

slime (SLIME)—a soft, slippery substance

trap (TRAP)—a method used to catch something

WATER POLLUTION

The sailors who dumped toxic waste into the sea in this book were polluting the water. Lots of different animals live in the seas and oceans, and many of them are hurt or killed by pollution every year. Some entire groups of animals are near extinction (ik-STINK-shuhn) because of pollution. A lot of water pollution comes from drains and sewers from the streets people live on. Most water pollution can be prevented — with a little work!

When people mow their lawns, lots of grass clippings are left in their yards and the streets. Grass clippings don't seem like they could harm animals, but they can be very harmful when they are swept into bodies of water through drains. When grass clippings are dumped into water, they suck up a lot of the water's oxygen. Fish need to breathe oxygen, just like humans do. When too many grass clippings get in the water, it sucks up too much oxygen, and fish die. You can help prevent this from happening. Tell your family and neighbors to keep grass clippings out of the street.

People use chemicals (KEM-ih-kuhlz) to clean cars, grow lawns, and kill bugs. All of these chemicals can make our lives better, but if people aren't careful with them, the chemicals can end up in the water. Chemicals get flushed into the water through drains, and they can hurt or kill animals that live in the water. The best way to prevent chemicals from harming the environment is to make sure that the products your family and friends use are safe for the environment.

Air pollution from cars is bad because it gets into the water. It's very unhealthy for animals and plants that live in the water. One way to cut down on air pollution is to ask family and friends to drive their cars less. Try walking, biking, or riding the bus more often.

We all need water to live. Make sure you do your part to keep our water healthy!

DISCUSSION QUESTIONS

1. The mutant jellyfish eat candy. Candy isn't a very healthy thing to eat in large amounts. What are some healthy snacks that the jellyfish, or you, could eat instead?

2. The sailors pollute the water and harm the jellyfish by dumping waste into the sea. What other things do humans do that is bad for water, nature, or animals? What can you do to help?

3. The sailors are punished by General Bullet for polluting the water. Do you think their punishment was fair? How should they have been punished?

WRITING PROMPTS

1. Billy Blaster and Wu Hoo battle mutant jellyfish. Write a story about you and your own mutant creature. Is it a good mutant or a bad mutant? Does it help people or just eat candy? You decide!

2. Billy Blaster and Wu Hoo are super heroes. If you were a super hero, what would your super powers be?

3. The sailors had to clean up the mess they made. Wu Hoo had to wash the dishes. Do you have to do chores? What kinds of chores? Write about your favorite and least favorite chores.

INTERNET SITES

Do you want to know more about subjects related to this book? Or are you interested in learning about other topics? Then check out FactHound, a fun, easy way to find Internet sites.

Our investigative staff has already sniffed out great sites for you!

Here's how to use FactHound:

1. Visit *www.facthound.com*

2. Select your grade level.

3. To learn more about subjects related to this book, type in the book's ISBN number: 9781434212696.

4. Click the Fetch It button.

FactHound will fetch the best Internet sites for you!